BILLIONAIRE COWBOY'S DREAM COME TRUE

Billionaire Cowboys of True Love, Texas, Book Five

HOPE MOORE

Billionaire Cowboy's Dream Come True

At long last Doctor Austin Tanner catches the garter at his brother's wedding while at the same time his gaze locks with a beautiful server watching him—the next moment she's down. All of his brothers believe after catching the garter he'll meet his match, just like all but one of them did. But not Austin—she's hurt and that's all he's thinking about as he rushes forward.

He's never totally believed as his brothers have that catching a garter led to them finding the loves of their lives.

Tess Piper has had a disastrous several months that led her to take the job as a server at weddings. She's lost so much in the last heartbreaking months and is trying to overcome it all by starting a new life in a new town where no one knows her. But the moment her gaze meets the handsome cowboy, who she'd also learned was a doctor, she freezes and then she falls…and when she opens her eyes, she finds the gorgeous doctor gazing down at her…and her life changes. Or it will if she lets it.

Once again, when these billionaire cowboys each catch a wedding garter, the next woman they meet is their one true-love.

Sounds simple but as always not so easy…

This is a smile worthy clean & wholesome romance series you'll love.

CHAPTER ONE

Austin Tanner watched his brother Jake smile as if he were the most blessed man in the world there in front of the church. Facing him, Hanna, the town veterinarian, smiled just as big and happily at him as the preacher presented them to the crowd as Mr. and Mrs. Jake Tanner.

The wedding crowd burst into applause, and Austin did also. He smiled happily for his brother, and at the exhilaration shining from his expression as he bent his head and kissed his bride with great enthusiasm. This had been a great day, and Austin was happy to see how extremely overjoyed Jake and Hanna were. Their joy was clear to everyone.

Austin still couldn't believe that all of his brothers had fallen in love and gotten married this last year to the first woman they'd seen or spoken to after catching the garter thrown at a wedding…all that is but Bret, who fell in love but not after the garter catch. After watching it happen to a couple of his brothers, Austin had thought it was suspicious and had started avoiding weddings. However, he couldn't avoid his brothers' weddings, so he'd kept his hands by his side, letting others grab the flying garter when it came into the group.

But, after watching his brothers Cole, Levi, and now Jake fall in love and marry the first woman they'd spoken to after catching the garter, he couldn't help being curious about what in the world was going on. And was this going to happen to him? It was a relief that Bret had broken the garter theory of his brothers because he didn't marry the first woman he locked eyes with after catching the garter.

But what about him…did he want it to happen to him?

Austin wasn't fighting it off if his time had arrived to find the love of his life, because his brothers were happy—extremely, passionately happy. But he was busy building his medical career and he still wasn't sure he was ready to fall in love. He hadn't even bought himself a house yet. He had moved out of the main house into one of the ranch's cabins after his older brother Cole had married Tulip and let the newlyweds have the main house. Levi and Bret had also done that earlier in the year, and now had gotten married and were building houses on the ranch with their wives. He hadn't known what his next step was going to be in his medical career until recently, so he remained in the cabin. Now, as he watched Hanna and Jake walk arm in arm down the aisle to the claps and cheers of everyone, his heart felt a pull of envy. It was the first time he'd had this feeling at any of his other brothers' weddings.

Everyone moved from the church to the tent out on the church's side lawn. Hanna had wanted the wedding to be in town like this, instead of at the ranch, because her customers were closer since they were in the large surrounding area of True Love, Texas. She was an excellent veterinarian, and everyone loved her. He was proud to call her his sister-in-law now.

Austin walked over to the drink table and picked up a glass of iced tea. He immediately took a drink and then watched the bride and groom happily visit with the line of attendees as the reception got underway.

He was happy for Jake and Hanna. Jake had been in love with Hanna from almost the moment she'd moved to town, but it had taken time for things to work out. It had taken awhile but he was really glad to see his brother happy.

"That went well," Bret said as he came up. "Are you ready to catch a garter here in a little bit?"

He'd known this was coming. His brothers assumed because he was the last one who was still single in the family that tonight he would catch the garter when Jake tossed it. Then he'd meet his wife and soon get married. Even though that hadn't happened to Bret, he believed it would for Austin.

Austin hitched a brow at his brother. "I told you and the others not to assume I'll be the one to catch this garter. I'm not avoiding them, but it will have to hit me directly in order for me to catch it. Just because the others caught one and then married the first woman they saw after that doesn't mean the garter caused it. You know that yourself. However, I'm not ready to test it out."

"But still, after catching it I fell in love. Don't we look happy?"

He grinned. "Y'all look very happy and I'm glad of that, but I'm not sure it's my time yet. Now with this move from the hospital emergency room to owning my own doctor's office in Fredericksburg, I've got a lot of adjusting to do. It's not the best time to start dating."

"I understand your thinking, and with your medical degree and talent you're probably smarter than any of us. However, when love happens, it happens and not in the moments you pick sometimes. So, if that garter comes at you, then catch it and see what happens. Believe us, you won't be sorry."

"I'd say if I reached for the garter and grabbed it when I wasn't supposed to, then it wouldn't count. But if it comes directly at me, I might. Besides, I'm still not convinced catching the garter was what got y'all married off, or if it was just a coincidence."

"Then catch it and see." Bret grinned in challenge.

He'd stepped into that. "Time to go visit with Mom and Dad and stop talking about me."

Bret hitched an eyebrow. "Fine. They probably want to tell you the same thing."

They headed toward their parents. They'd made it in for the wedding tonight and would leave on a cruise tomorrow. His parents had worked hard on the ranch for years and hadn't traveled much before they'd struck the abundance of oil a few years ago that had changed all of their lives. His parents almost immediately handed the ranch over to him and his brothers; they'd retired, bought an ocean-view home in Florida, and started traveling while their sons took over ranching.

He and his brothers were happy for them and enjoyed seeing them when they made it to town.

"Mom, Dad, it was great, wasn't it?" He pushed thoughts of the garter out of his mind. If he was to fall in love, he would, and a garter had nothing to do with it.

His mother's eyes lit up. "It was wonderful. Now, we're excited to see you catch the garter and fall in love too."

Maybe he should head home now. The expectations for him tonight were getting out of hand.

* * *

Server Tess Piper carried the tray of bacon-wrapped

appetizers on a tray as all the men were called to gather in a group for the garter toss. She'd reached the internal edge of the crowd and had a good view as the groom turned his back, ready to throw the garter. Tess froze, not wanting to be the only one moving around as he threw it over his shoulder. Her gaze went to the men but was caught instantly on the groom's brother, whom she had noticed the minute he'd walked into the reception tent. Austin was so handsome, with his short, dark hair and darker blue eyes and a jawline she suddenly wanted to trace with her fingertips. *What was she thinking?*

Earlier she had asked one of the other waitresses who he was and been told he was Austin, the brother of the groom, and a doctor who'd just taken over a doctor's office on the outskirts of Fredericksburg. She'd tried not to but found herself watching him off and on all evening as she walked around. He looked like a nice guy but, of course, she told herself to get her eyes off the man because she was here to do her job.

She was here to rebuild her life.

And that did not mean with a man.

But now, she had locked eyes with him as Jake

threw the garter over his shoulders. She couldn't look away from the cowboy doctor as he held her gaze, as if he couldn't look away either. She gasped as the garter hit Austin in the face.

He jumped, yanked his gaze off her, and miraculously caught the garter as it fell toward the floor. She was intrigued at how startled the man was, looking at the piece of ribbon in his hand. Obviously, he hadn't been in the group to actually catch the garter. To her surprise, he was looking at her again, his eyes drilling into her with intensity. Startled, she stepped back just as she was bumped hard from behind, sending the tray of food in her hand flying as she stumbled forward. Her feet flew up behind her as she fell forward toward the floor. She reached out with her hands, trying to stop herself from slamming into the hard floor. Her hand hit first, and she screamed as her body followed. Unable to move in that moment as the pain throbbed, she just laid there, fighting off tears.

Someone's gentle hands took her shoulders and carefully rolled her onto her back. And she found herself staring through tear-filled eyes into the close-up, worried eyes of Austin Tanner.

Oh goodness, he was so gorgeous. And even though she was hurting with pain, she could see how his eyes were full of concern.

"Just lay still. I'm a doctor, so let me check you out." His gaze raked over her body and then came back to stare into her eyes. "Are you hurting anywhere other than your wrist that you're holding?"

She couldn't move and at the moment didn't want to. "Just my wrist. My knees a little." She fought off the tears and stared at her hand instead of his eyes.

He had taken her hand into his and was gently touching the swelling wrist with his finger. "Your wrist is probably either sprained or broken. Are you sure you aren't hurting anywhere else?"

"I think that's all."

"Then let's try to sit you up and let me look at your wrist." He eased her up to a sitting position. "Can you sit up on your own while I look at your wrist?"

She nodded, and he let go of her shoulders and gently took her hand into his hand.

Everyone who was gathered around them did not

interrupt him as he checked out her arm and wrist. His fingers were gentle but when he touched a spot on her wrist, she cried out softly, unable to stop herself.

His concerned gaze met hers. "I think you're going to have to have an x-ray. I have a machine at my office on the outer edge of Fredericksburg, so let me help you up and I'll take you there for one."

She did not want to have a broken wrist at all. It would not help her. "But this is your brother's wedding." She felt horrible, taking him away from the celebration.

"It's almost over. They're going to dance and then they're going to head off for their honeymoon. We're just leaving a bit early. Okay?"

The groom stepped out of the crowd behind her, where she hadn't been able to see him. Now, Jake looked kindly down at her. "Austin is the best man to take care of you, and we are grateful and totally support his stepping in to take care of you. So please let him."

Her gaze shifted from the groom back to the doctor. "Okay then, thank you." Despite the aching of her wrist, looking into the kind doctor's eyes instantly caused her heart to cinch dramatically. And when he smiled…she knew it was going to be hard to ignore, but it would be ignored.

"Great. Now let's get you up and to my truck, and then the office. Can you tell me your name?" He gently put his arm around her waist and helped her stand.

She had to say, if anybody in the whole room was going to put their arm around her and help her stand, this was the man she would have picked. She met his gaze. "I'm Tess Piper. And thank you."

"Tess, I'm just glad I'm here to help you."

Her boss moved to stand beside them. "Austin, we can take her to the hospital."

"Thanks, Tim, but I insist," Austin said without hesitation.

"Then, thank you." Tim looked at her. "Let me know what you find out. Here's the insurance information just in case you don't have your purse with you."

She took it in her free hand. "Thank you. This will help."

Austin started leading her as he kept his arm around

her waist. "No need for that. This x-ray is going to be free to you."

She looked up at him, her heart pounding. "Thank you." She would have loved to say no, and insist she pay her own bills…but she knew that right now, she couldn't.

Not until she got her feet and her life back on the ground.

CHAPTER TWO

Minutes later, Austin helped the beautiful Tess into his truck. His brother Cole had pulled it into the circle drive while he led her outside. On the way out, everyone wished her luck and thanked her for being a waitress at the wedding. Jake and Hanna had both thanked her for helping with their wedding and told her they were so sorry to see her suffering. She had managed a weak smile, but he could tell by the look in her eyes that she was hurting, so he'd take care of her, and thankfully they relaxed because they knew he would.

He helped her step up into the truck's passenger seat and buckled her in. Then he'd strode quickly around the truck and slid in behind the steering wheel. Seeing her expression of pain, he reached into the backseat of the truck and grabbed his emergency bag. He pulled out a bottle of prescription painkiller—just a bit stronger than a regular strength—and then he grabbed a bottle of unopened water he kept there for emergencies. He opened it and held both out to her.

"What is it?" she asked.

"Painkiller. Not the kind that'll knock you out but the kind to level out the pain you're experiencing."

Her expression was thankful. "Thank you. I need this so much." She quickly swallowed the painkiller with a swallow of water.

No doubt about it; she was hurting. He didn't like that. She must have hit on that floor just right and he had a bad feeling she could have a broken wrist. It could be sprained, though; that, too, could be extremely painful but most of the time would heal quicker. Thankfully they would know soon.

Moments later, they were headed toward Fredericksburg and his new office. The recent decision to stop his emergency room work and finally open his own practice had been a fast decision when the physician who had been their family doctor as he'd grown up had called and told him he was retiring. Doctor Perry had made an unbelievably low offer for him to take over his practice because he wanted to sell it to Austin, whom he trusted to take care of his beloved patients. The office was on the outskirts of Fredericksburg, making it quick access for people who lived out of the in-town area. And to him, considering he still lived on the ranch outside of True Love, which was thirty miles from the medical office.

Austin felt honored by Dr. Perry's offer and realized it was exactly what he wanted and bought it within two weeks. He'd gone to work with Dr. Perry immediately, who stuck around for a couple of weeks to help him settle in. Also, so he could say goodbye to his patients and so that he could introduce Austin to as many of them as he could. It had shown Austin that this was what he wanted: patients who he cared for and who cared for him. This was the way he could eventually settle down and be ready when he did fall in love and get married. He wasn't ready yet, but he was ready to get prepared and that idea alone made him happy.

"You are very welcome. I'm glad to have been

there to help you and feel bad that it happened during that distracting garter toss." He didn't go further with his thoughts. *The garter toss when his gaze snagged onto hers and she didn't look away and then slipped and fell.* He wasn't sure what had happened in that moment when their gazes locked, but he felt responsible for her accident.

Tess blinked at him, looking very emotional. "It wasn't your fault. I wasn't paying attention to what I was doing."

He reached over with his right hand and touched her good arm. "It was just an accident. I saw you fall, after our gazes met, and I think there was just a lot going on around you when you lost balance and fell forward." *There, hopefully that helped without going deeper into the fact that neither of them had been paying attention to anything but each other.*

"Maybe so." She leaned her head back and closed her eyes.

They drove in silence for a few minutes. Then his curiosity took over. "This company you work for at the wedding tonight has done several other weddings for us and events that I've been to in the last several months. I haven't seen you at any of those. Are you new in town?"

She opened her eyes, met his, and then looked down at her hands. "Yes. I moved here less than two months ago. I live in a small rental outside of Fredericksburg. I was glad to get this job and never even thought about being injured."

"I don't think accidents happen often at the restaurant, so hopefully after you get well, you'll be fine. It seems like a good company to work for, since everybody seems to be content there. My sister-in-law and her two partners host weddings and parties and use them often. Hopefully Tim will be able to keep you working, even if your wrist is broken."

Tess looked his way just as he'd glanced from the road back to her. "I've worked several parties and weddings this last month. Maybe it's because it's spring. But I have no idea what will happen now."

Austin saw the worry in her eyes in the brief moments he'd looked at her. Now he stared out at the road, his mind working. He glanced at her; she'd leaned her head back and had her eyes closed again. Hopefully the painkiller was working now. One thing he was sure of: if she lost her job, he'd make sure she found a new one.

* * *

They arrived at the red brick building and were inside within moments, and he'd x-rayed Tess's aching wrist. Now she watched him study the black-and-white photo.

He turned toward her, looking relieved. "Your wrist isn't broken."

At Austin's words, her eyes filled with tears of relief. "Wonderful," she gasped.

He smiled but continued to look concerned. "Yes, but you have a very sprained situation. Let's get it wrapped up, get two more non-prescription ibuprofen for a painkiller to see if that's enough to kill the pain, and then I'll get you home so you can get some sleep. Since it's not a worse sprain, that painkiller should be fine, but we'll see."

"Thank you for doing all this for me." Relief continued washing through her. She knew sprains could take a while to heal, but she was going to think positive about it. "I'm relieved to know that it's not broken and just hope that it doesn't take a long time to heal."

He had sat down on a stool and started wrapping her arm in a flexible bandage. "It's going to heal, but you still need at least a week off. Maybe more. And until I tell you it's ready, you can't use it. Maybe your boss will be able to use you with only the use of one arm for one to two weeks. Or the small possibility of more."

She stared at him. He was clearly hating telling her this, and she hated hearing it. "I'll figure something out. Thankfully it wasn't broken and it's not my handwriting hand, so maybe I can do something in the restaurant office for a short time."

"Maybe so." He continued wrapping her hand, wrist, and forearm. "If something happens and they can't keep you working, I can help get you a different job. I could even hire you to help out in the office here. And then, if you prefer the other job, when your wrist is healed, they'd probably hire you back."

"Giving me a job is not your responsibility. You've already helped me tremendously. Just with this free x-ray and bandaging—" She swallowed hard, her nerves rattling with emotion. "I'm not in my best situation financially right now. And I wasn't sure if my boss covered the bill upfront or replaced my money later, if at all. No need to worry, I'll figure out my next step." She fought hard to sound positive and hoped he thought the slight tremor in her voice was from the pain.

He finished the wrap, stood up, and carried the supplies to the cabinet, and put them back where they'd been before he turned and looked at her. "I want to make sure you have the money you need. And like I said, I will gladly hire you to help in my office. I meant my offer and I do need help. But think about it, and I'll check with you tomorrow. Right now, I'm getting you home so you can get some rest."

"Sounds good," she said weakly.

He helped her up and they walked out of the building, where he helped her back into the passenger seat. Then he stretched the seat belt across her and secured it. She stared at him, unable to take her eyes off his handsome face. His eyes dug into hers, sending shivers racing through her, even though she knew she had to ignore the attraction she felt for him.

She had lost her previous life and was still trying to adjust to her loss. She'd just been basically broke moneywise and heartbroken, too, when she drove into Fredericksburg. It was a nice area and with the town's sightseers and wine tour traffic, she felt positive she could find a job. She found a cheap motel for the night and began her search immediately. Luck had been on her side and the next morning, she found a job as a waitress and then a cheap, tiny place on the outskirts of town.

It wasn't fancy, not at all, but it was all she could afford or needed at this time. She just needed a place to work and to find her way again, and the rundown house worked for now.

Especially considering having this injury might hurt her ability with her job. She had to have money coming in, or she was in trouble. The worry was starting to overtake her, even though if she were lucky, her recovery would only be a week or two at the most.

She concentrated on telling him where her rental house was instead of what would happen if she had to be off work very long. Within just a very few minutes, Austin pulled into the driveway. He said nothing about the rundown house as he parked. Instead, he cut the engine off, grabbed the keys as he rammed his door open, jumped out, and slammed it behind him as he jogged around the truck to her. In shock, she watched his actions.

"Let me help you," he said, as he opened her door. "You look very disoriented, like the pain medicine is affecting you."

Astonished by his quickness, she reached out to take his hand, realizing he was right; she was unsteady. "Was the last medicine different?"

"Yes. I decided to give you a prescription painkiller, slightly stronger than the non-prescription. I wanted to get you home, in bed, and hopefully you'd sleep most of the night. I sensed you might need some help because you were looking so worried."

"I'm worried about getting inside right now."

"I've got you." He helped her climb from the truck; slid an arm around her waist, and held her steady as they moved to the front door.

She had told him earlier that the door key was on her car's key ring, which he had slipped into his pocket. He pulled the ring out and had the key ready when they reached the door and quickly had it swinging open. Tess was a little wobbly as he led her into the combination tiny living room and kitchen. She saw him glance around at the old couch and chair and a small kitchen table the house had come with, which was good considering she had no furniture of her own. The couch and chair were old, but as clean as she could make them. She had scrubbed them down with a cleanser and then vacuumed them several times. There was a bathroom in the tiny hall leading to the single bedroom, and she needed it.

"I need to go to the bathroom. She leaned her head on his shoulder as her knees weakened slightly.

"Okay, then it's to bed for you." He led her into the bathroom. "Can you make it on your own?"

"I'm fine. Go." She placed her hands on the counter and he left the room, pulling the door closed. She stared at herself in the mirror. She looked horrible. Then she turned away and took care of business. Hopefully, after some sleep, she would be more normal tomorrow.

* * *

Austin strode to the kitchen, opened the cabinets, and found a glass, then an ice tray in the old refrigerator's freezer. He plunked out a few cubes into the glass, then filled it with water. He had just set the glass on the bedside table when he heard the door open to the bathroom.

He spun just as she came out, holding onto the doorframe. "Hang on." He rushed to her side and slid his arm around her back. "Are you okay?"

"I'm still wobbly."

"I'm here to help." He helped her to the bed. "What can I get you to sleep in?"

"That top drawer of that chest." She nodded at the cream-toned chest of drawers. "There is a cotton shirt and some warmup pants."

As he opened the drawer and pulled out the items, it dawned on him that she was going to have trouble getting the shirt on. He turned around. "Are you going to have trouble getting this on?"

"No, it stretches. As long as I put the wrapped arm through the sleeve before I put the other one in, then I'll manage."

"Sounds like you have a plan. I'll leave the room."

"You can go ahead and go home. There's no sense me stealing any more of your night."

"I'll be here when you're changed." He pulled the door closed and walked out before she could say anything. There was no way he was leaving until she was safely in bed and her eyes were closed. And even then, he was going to have a hard time making himself leave.

CHAPTER THREE

Sunday morning, sparkling sunlight shone through the living room as Tess walked down the hall to the kitchen. Her wrist still throbbed but not like it had before. She had no painkiller in her now and hoped the over-the-counter ibuprofen she had would be enough, because she wasn't going to be like she'd been last night. First, she needed coffee, so she headed to the coffeepot and saw a note beside it.

Good morning, Tess. Hope you are better. Just push start and coffee will begin brewing. Talk to you soon, Austin.

Shocked, she smiled as she pushed the black button and immediately heard it begin to brew. He had been wonderful the night before, taking care of her and hating to leave until she was sleeping. Obviously, she had fallen asleep and he'd left at some point, but getting coffee ready for her had been so very thoughtful. *Did it show that he really cared about her?*

She pushed that thought away. That was not something she needed to think about. He cared because he was acting as her doctor, and that was the way she needed to look at it.

She needed to get her wrist healed, get back to working, and get her new life started again. Losing her parents had been horrible. Add to that the fact she'd pretty much lost everything of her own out of stupidity and been forced to move from Houston to her parents' home to live because of that. And then they had their accident. She took a deep breath, reminding herself that moving home had been a blessing, putting her there for her dad before he died. So a personal bad choice had put her where she needed to be, close to her dying dad after losing her mother.

Her heart hurt so badly that she never planned to love or trust anyone ever again.

Betrayal hurt bad enough, but losing loved ones hurt far greater.

She grabbed two ibuprofens from the bottle sitting on the counter and took them with the bit of water she put in her mug. She poured the rest out, then she filled the mug full of coffee, carried it to the table and sat in one of the chairs by the window. She took a sip of the hot liquid and let the scent and taste radiate through her. She took another one and closed her eyes, taking it all in and waiting for the pain medicine to work. The sound of a vehicle outside had her eyes reopening to see Austin in his truck, sitting outside the window. And he was smiling at her.

Tess's heart began to pound. She stood and moved to open the door for him as he climbed from the truck. "Good morning," she said, feeling much better seeing him.

"Good morning to you. Are you feeling better? You look much better than you did last night."

"Yes, I am. My arm still hurts but not as bad as it hurt last night, thanks to you."

"I'm glad I could help. Now, can I come in and take a look at the injury? Grab a cup of coffee, too?"

"Of course. Please come in. I just woke up and have

only had two sips myself."

"Then sit back down and drink a little more. I'll get my own cup and join you."

She closed the door after him and did just as he suggested. Moments later, he sat in the other chair and took his own first sip of coffee while she took another.

"Thank you for all you did last night." Tess set her cup down, feeling overpowered with gratefulness to him.

"Okay, stop. You don't have to thank me anymore. I'm glad I was able to help you and that you weren't hurt worse. Have you taken some over-the-counter ibuprofen this morning? I left some on the counter for you in case you didn't have any."

"Yes, I took two, and it's starting to ease the pain. I think it will be enough."

"Good, but just let me know if it isn't." He held his hand out. "Let me feel it."

She placed her hand in his, and he gently moved his other hand over the bandage, touching certain areas. She winced slightly but not wildly.

"I think it's fine. If you feel like you can drive with

one hand, then I'll take you to pick up your car. But if not, then I'll get one of my brothers to go with me to pick it up."

"I want to say I can drive, but at the moment I'm not sure."

Austin watched her with penetrating eyes, and he nodded at her words. "Then I'll call Cole, and we'll pick it up after he gets out of church with Tulip, his wife. They live on the ranch near True Love, so it'll be early afternoon probably before he can get here."

"I hate to do that to them. I might be able to drive. Let me go get dressed, move around a little, and I can try. It's not that far away and it will feel better to me if I at least try." And it was the truth. She wanted to take care of her own needs.

"Only if you want to. I'll drink my coffee while you move around and get dressed. We'll go from there."

"I'll be back." She stood and felt more confident because she wasn't wobbly like last night. It was just the idea of her hand in a wrap. But her fingers moved, so maybe she could do it. She headed down the hall. If he was willing to help her like he was, then she was going to give her side of the bargain everything she could.

* * *

Thirty minutes later, Austin drove down the road with Tess in the passenger seat. Today, she was in much better shape than last night. He should have told her not to try this, but he had the feeling that she would have been upset. The restaurant wasn't opening until later, so it would be easy to have her drive around in the parking lot, so they'd get a feeling for her ability. Either way, it was getting her moving around and out of the house for a little while.

And if he were honest with himself, it gave them more time together. "How's your pain? Is the ibuprofen working well enough?"

She cringed slightly. "It's working good enough, but the pain is very evident. But I don't want to take anything stronger because I need to be able to think and function."

"I understand. Have you given any thought to working at the office this coming week?" She'd turned him down last night, yet he felt drawn to ask again now that she wasn't on the harder medicine and she had slept.

"I don't know. I really appreciate the offer, but I hate to be a hardship on you."

He pulled into the restaurant's parking lot that had one small car in it. He drove toward the older car and then stopped before he spoke. "Honestly, I need the extra help. I was getting ready to put an ad out." They stared at each other, and he couldn't shut down the way his attraction to her intensified. "I'm serious, Tess. You'd be helping me out."

Her eyes softened. "If that's the case, the real case, then I'm grateful for the opportunity and accept. I have a feeling the restaurant won't have a use for me right now, no matter how I was counting on it."

His heart jumped at her words. "Then I thank you. And my receptionist thanks you. Now, let's get out and take a quick spin in the parking lot and judge if you can handle the driving."

"I can do this." She pushed the seat belt release button with her left hand, then reached across her body to open the door and pushed it open with her foot.

"Hang on," he said, but she was already standing beside the truck, much quicker than she'd been moving last night, so that was a good thing. He jumped out his side, slammed the door, and met her beside the car. He pulled out the car keys and pushed the unlock on the button. "Let me get the door for you." He smiled and pulled the door open. She immediately slid into the seat, but he didn't miss the cringe on her face and knew her arm hadn't liked her movement.

"Keys, please." She held out her good hand.

Feeling uncertain about her next actions, he held onto the keys, gently closed the door, then strode around the car and slid into the passenger's seat with her staring at him. He held them out to her. "You can have them now. I wasn't sure if you were going to drive off and leave me, and I want to be certain you can do this."

"Fine. You've been great, so I wouldn't have done that to you."

He smiled and was glad; he believed her, from the look in her pretty blue eyes. "Sorry, I'm just being cautious."

He watched as she awkwardly reached around the

steering wheel and cranked the car with her left hand and then smiled at him. "I will be cautious, too. I promise. And yes, that move right there was a little tough because even though I'm left handed I usually start the car with my right hand and work the gearshift too."

"You did good." He smiled at her and she looked pleased.

They both put their seat belts on and then she put her foot on the brake while she used her left hand to reach across to the gearshift that was between the seats. She pulled it into the drive position, then grabbed the steering wheel with her left hand and gently placed the fingertips of her bandaged right hand on it also.

He thought she'd done a great job so far.

"Here we go," she said, softly, as she pulled her foot from the brake and pressed the gas pedal gently, then drove forward slowly in the empty parking lot.

"You're doing good," he said, hoping this wasn't too hard on her wrist.

She turned the car before reaching the end of the parking lot and didn't say anything, so he asked, "Is it feeling okay?"

She beamed at him. "Yes, it is. I can make it back to the house. Do you want to lead or follow?" She pulled to a halt beside his truck and did a good job.

"I'll lead and keep an eye on you behind me." He could choose the speed that way, just in case if she led, she got the desire to test her speed.

"Very well. I guess I won't race back today." She winked at him as if she'd read his mind.

"Thank goodness." He laughed, drawn more to her now than before…and that was already a lot.

About six minutes later, they were back at her house. He wasn't ready to leave her. She'd driven well and she was coming to work tomorrow, so he would be able to check her out then. So there was no reason for him not to leave. Except that he just wasn't ready.

He climbed out of the truck and he walked to the car as she pulled in beside him. He opened the door and instantly could tell she was hurting. He reached for her good arm and helped her stand up. "It looks like it's time for a little rest. Promise me you're not going to be driving anymore today. And if you need me to pick you up on my way to the office in the morning at eight o'clock, I can do it. If that's not too early for you. I'm not seeing patients until nine."

She gave him a slightly weak smile. "I'll be fine. It just hurt a bit moving, from my fingers pressing on the steering wheel. I've not pressed them or strained them until now. It will get better."

"I'll come in and make you an ice pack for you to use. That will help. Keep the ice tray creating new ice, and do it every couple of hours at least."

"I will, and I can put ice in a towel." She then paused, her expression falling. "I just realized I can't get ice out of the ice trays with only one hand."

"Then I'll fix you up. I'll empty those four trays into a bowl so you can get them out with one hand. And you shouldn't take too many at a time. Tomorrow, at work, I have ice bags you can use, and I'll send some home that you can pull out of the freezer and use for the rest of the time."

"Thank you again." She smiled then pressed the key into the door and opened it.

"I'm glad to help. And I mean it, Tess."

She sank down on the couch while he got the first ice pack wrapped in a cloth and took it to her. Then he went back, and emptied the other trays and slipped the big bowl into the freezer. Something told him not to baby her because he could tell she was embarrassed.

He moved back to where she sat. "Okay, is it starting to work?"

"Yes. I'll be fine. I'll see you in the morning."

He hated leaving her, though he knew it was time. "Call if you need anything—wait," he gasped as it hit him. "Food. Do you have food you can prepare with your hurt arm?"

"I have one not-hurt arm with a very good hand attached. I can prepare whatever I want to eat. I'm fine now."

"Then I'm fine now too. See you tomorrow." With that, Austin forced himself to open the door, wave as he locked it, then closed it behind him, and made himself go get in his truck.

And drive away.

He would see her tomorrow. Hopefully her injury would heal quickly, and the pain and worry he saw in her expression would go away as she would be able to get back to her regular job if she wanted it. He wondered what Tess's story was.

Because something deep inside him told him there was a story.

CHAPTER FOUR

The next morning, Tess eased her car into a parking space at the back of the office's parking lot. She worked here and didn't plan to take up a closer space that a patient could want. Austin's truck was parked by the back door, where a sign claimed it for him. She understood why; he was the doctor and might need to get in fast to help someone or get out fast to get to the hospital for someone. She was not him and took nothing for granted. Even these tingles that raced through her just thinking about him.

He had helped her and that was her excuse for the way she reacted to thoughts of him. Nothing more. Nothing.

He had told her to come in the back entrance, so she walked past his truck and pulled the heavy metal door open with her good hand, just like he'd done when he'd brought her the other night. There was soft music playing and at the end of the hall was a dark-haired woman who looked about fifty.

She smiled when she saw Tess and hurried down the hall toward her. "Tess. I'm Ramona Bell. I run the office and am thrilled to have some help."

Feeling totally welcomed by the lady, Tess smiled. "I'm thrilled to help. Did Austin tell you that I'm one-handed at the moment?"

"Yes, I did," Austin said as he came out of an office at the end of the hall. "Sorry to miss introducing you two. I was caught on a call. I think you'll get along well. Tess, Ramona will get you started."

The back door opened, and they all glanced that way to see a pretty blonde woman about Tess's age enter. "Good morning, everyone." She smiled. "Sorry I'm a touch late. Got caught in traffic near the nursery, dropping off Lila. Hi, you must be our new helper."

Austin grinned. "Kimberly, this is Tess Piper. Tess, Kimberly is my nurse, and I told her you were coming too."

"Hello." Tess held her fingers out before thinking about her hurt wrist. "Sorry for the awkward shake," she said, realizing what she'd done.

Kimberly lightly touched her fingers without shaking them. Obviously, being a nurse, she knew not to shake. "Austin sent me a text about hiring you and about your wrist being hurt. I'm sorry, but even one-handed you'll still be a great help to Ramona."

"Yes, she will be," Ramona said. "They need to get ready for patients so if you'll follow me, I'll get you started. This is going to be perfect."

Tess smiled at Austin and Kimberly. "Work calls," she said, then followed Ramona up front into the office area.

"I'll be checking on your wrist in a little bit," Austin said.

She looked over her shoulder. "It's fine right now. Took my over-the-counter painkillers and doing better today."

He gave her a nod. "That's good to hear."

Tess watched as he and Kimberly headed down the hall, then she continued to the front office.

Ramona was smiling at her and waved her toward a desk that was beside a wall of files. "This is where you'll work most of the time. We have all these files that need to be filed online. I worked for the last doctor here for fifteen years and just didn't have his stuff uploaded. He was older and from a different time. But times have changed, and it needs to be done as Dr. Tanner begins his journey with his patients, and he knows he'll have to adapt his office to the future. Therefore, this small office is going to grow under his great skills. He's planning to bring in other doctors as he goes. Therefore, I desperately needed help, and he brought you in to help me."

"And it really does sound like you need help. I hope I'm good enough." Tess glanced at all the file cabinets, drew in a determined breath and looked back to Ramona. "I can do this, slower than if I had two hands, but I promise I'll get it done for you. Just tell me how and what exactly you need. Austin—I mean, Dr. Tanner—helped my hurt hand, so I can do whatever you need or he needs."

Ramona winked at her. "I had a feeling you could."

In the next couple of minutes, she explained what she needed done, and then the phone rang and the front door opened, and a lady and a child came inside. "It's open time, so this is all yours. I'll be right over there if you need to ask me anything." She smiled then strode over and answered the phone as she sank into her rolling office chair. She had a three-sided desk, with a large side for a computer and files, a side that had a sliding glass window to the waiting room, and a side that faced the area where they'd been standing earlier to take the patients' money before they exited. And she looked totally capable of handling her area.

Tess took a deep breath again, determined she could handle her area also and help Ramona. She sat down in her rolling chair and went to work at her desk that faced the wall. Her wrist hurt some, but she could easily do this filing job. However, looking at how many there were, she had no idea how long it would take.

* * *

It was close to lunch before Austin had a few moments

free to check on Tess, and he was ready to make sure she was handling the work okay. He walked into the front office and saw her with her back to him, copying an old file into the copy machine, sending them to the computer file. "Tess, do you have a moment to let me look at your wrist?"

She looked over her shoulder at him. "Sure. I'm fine, though."

"I just want to see if the swelling is going down."

She stood and followed him across the hallway to where he held the door for her to enter the exam room.

"Just sit in the chair instead of the examination table."

"Sure." She sat as he pulled his rolling stool over and sat in front of her.

"Your hand, please." He took her hand, noticing the swelling of her fingers had lessened. "Is it feeling better? The work's not causing it to hurt worse?" He met her gaze, instantly feeling the warmth of her blue eyes.

"It's better. If it keeps this up every day, then I feel positive I'll be back to normal quickly. Thank goodness."

"Yes, you will be. I'm glad too, though I can already tell Ramona will miss you."

"She's really great."

"I agree with you. And you're great, helping us out. If you change your mind about going back to your other job, this one is yours…and with benefits and raises." He realized he hadn't told her that before now. And he suddenly hoped it helped her decide to stay.

Ramona had come back earlier to bring a file for a patient to him, and she'd told him he needed to hang on to Tess. That had been all the recommendation he needed to offer Tess the job.

"Thank you for the offer. I like Ramona, too, and though I just met Kimberly briefly, she seems really nice also."

"She is, and I hope you think the same thing about me." Austin smiled, realizing he was still holding her arm carefully.

Tess's pretty eyes sparkled. "I do. And it's easy to tell the patients like you also. I've heard several tell Ramona as they are paying that they are glad you took over the practice."

"I like them too. I'm glad I made this decision to move out of the emergency room. I'm enjoying the idea of helping people stay out of the hospital, if possible. Okay, so keep the job in mind, and tomorrow I'll change that wrap and give you a fresh one." He didn't want to let go of her hand. But he knew he had to, so he gently placed it on her thigh. He'd made his offer of the permanent job and hoped she decided to stay.

"Can I go back to work?"

"Yes, or it may be time for you to eat. Ask Ramona."

Austin watched her leave and was still unable to shake the attraction he felt for her. He wasn't sure whether she felt anything for him other than gratefulness for taking care of her injury and the job.

He had a busy afternoon and didn't get to talk to her again as he went from one room to the next, seeing patients. The office closed at four o'clock, but most times he was behind a little and had some paperwork to catch up on. Today, it was almost six when he finished his reports and he'd been on the phone when Ramona had stuck her head in the door and waved, meaning they were leaving. He lifted a hand in good-bye as the doctor he was consulting with on the phone continued talking. He had hoped to get to see how Tess had held up for the day, but this was an important call. Hopefully she'd made it all right.

* * *

Tess pushed her good hand, the left one, through the gap of the steering wheel and tried to start the engine again. But again, it just clicked. She cringed, then pulled her hand back and rubbed her forehead. Her battery had finally gone dead. Kimberly had left earlier to pick up her child, and Ramona had just left as Tess was getting into her car. And now she was having trouble with her car. The only person left at the office was Austin. He had been on a medical call when they'd left moments ago, and she didn't want to go back inside and bother him. She also didn't know who to call, didn't yet have the extra money to pay anyone…so she was in trouble again.

She hated this. She dropped her forehead to the

back of her good hand that now gripped the steering wheel. *What if it wasn't the battery but was something worse, more expensive for this aging car?* Before he died, her sweet daddy had insisted she keep his truck once he was dead. He'd been worried about her, which was so like him. But he had no idea that his and her mother's car wreck had cost them everything: her mother's life, their small house that she had to sell to pay her dad's medical bills as he struggled to live. And then his truck, which had to be sold to pay for his funeral. Her heart thundered as all the harsh pain of the last year came out to haunt her.

A tap on her window had her yanking her head up and staring into Austin's eyes.

"Tess, what's wrong?" he said, loud enough for her to hear through the glass. Then he pulled the door open and knelt beside her.

He was such a wonderful man. "My car won't start and I'm worried that it might be more than just a dead battery."

Relief replaced his worried expression. "I'm glad it isn't your wrist. Pop the hood and let me take a look. I have a battery charger in my truck, and we'll test it out and see if it starts."

Relief washed through her. "Thank you. I wasn't sure what I was going to do, and I didn't want to come in and bother you again."

He smiled gently at her. "You aren't bothering me." He reached in beside her leg and popped the small lever that released the hood. He stood and strode to the front of the car, and lifted the hood up.

She got out and moved to stand beside him as he gave the engine a quick glance-over.

"Let me get my truck pulled over here, and let's hook our batteries together and see if we can charge yours up."

His words were completely innocent, but her heart skipped as she watched him cross the parking lot to his truck. Everything about her was now charged up. Except her car. She couldn't let these feelings he caused in her to take over. She stepped away from the car as he pulled his truck up close, then jumped out and lifted his hood. He then opened the door to the backseat on the driver's side and came out carrying a red-and-blue wired cabled battery charger.

"Let's see what happens. If you'll go back to the driver's seat, I'll let you know when to start it again."

"Thanks. Will do." She hurried back and took her position. In a moment, he looked around the hood and gave her a thumbs-up. With a quick prayer, she turned the key. The engine roared to life. Relief poured over her, and she jumped from the car and rushed forward as he came toward her with a huge smile. Without thinking, she threw her good arm around his neck and held on in a one-armed hug. "Thank you. That seems to be all I say to you." She buried her face in his shoulder and fought down the tears of gratefulness overwhelming her.

He had wrapped his arms around her, and one hand gently rubbed her hair while the other her back. "I've been completely happy to help. You are a lovely lady, Tess."

His tender voice and words added more leverage to the need to cry. After losing her parents and having no one, she felt heavily overwhelmed to feel his kindness. And the gentle touch of his hands trying to comfort her.

"Are you all right?" he asked when she remained quiet.

Biting her lip, she lifted her face from his shoulder. "Yes," she managed. "I just got overwhelmed by your actions." Her gaze dropped to his lips before she could stop them and when she instantly forced them back to his eyes, she saw his own attraction to her light up in them. *Was he going to kiss her?* She told herself to back away, but she was unable to move.

His head dipped toward her; her pulse skyrocketed. And then he paused and stepped back, and her pulse rolled downhill.

"I've been glad to help. You seem to have no one, and it worries me. Tell me I'm wrong."

Tess took a deep breath. "I have no one close to me. I had been working as a secretary at a large distribution company in Houston, but then had to move home. My mother and dad had a major car wreck…my sweet mother was killed instantly. My poor father was injured terribly. He had broken both his legs, one crushed, and he'd also had his stomach and other organs damaged and had to have several surgeries. And then fight for his life. Not only was he fighting to survive the surgeries, but infections began to fight to take him. He died about four weeks after the wreck. He had desperately needed me while he was fighting for his life, and I was so glad I was able to be there with him. He was lost in mourning for my mother and blamed himself for her death. To be honest, it was his fault, and there was no denying it. But she would have forgiven him for running off the road and then such disaster happening."

Thinking of her lost mother and her father's broken heart had her looking away, out toward the shops farther down the street. *Why had she opened up like this to him?*

"You've had a terribly sad year. I'm so sorry," he said gently.

His words touched her with the depth of his tone.

She met his concerned gaze. "Thank you for your understanding. I have to move on, but it's been hard. Waiting on people at weddings shouldn't have made me feel better. I just took the job because it was open and soon realized walking around, serving happy people at the parties, lifted my spirits. Helped me know that new life stories were starting every day. Maybe mine would be soon. Not me getting married, but being able to let go of the sadness of my past and move forward."

His eyes warmed and he cocked his lips in a smile. "You'll do that. I know you will. And Tess, thank you for sharing this with me. I've been thinking you had something holding you down. And it worried me."

"You were right. You always seem to be right."

"I'm not always so on target, but there is just something about you that reaches out at me. Now, your car needs to have a new battery. That one may not start again tomorrow. How about we go down to the auto shop and we get you one and I'll install it?"

"To be honest, until I get a paycheck in a few days, I don't have the money. The money I have is already spent, paying rent and for the electric bill. I just have a little left and that won't be enough to pay for a battery." Being honest was all she had right now.

"Then I'll buy it and put it in. And if you won't accept it as a gift, then I'll take it out of your check at the end of the week. How is that?"

She wished she wasn't in this situation, but she was, and no way did she want to miss work tomorrow because her car refused to start. "Thank you for the offer, and I'll gladly accept paying you from my check."

He smiled. "Great. Let me unhook the truck from the car and then follow me, and we'll get this fixed."

"You are a miracle worker to me."

He smiled. "Never been called that before but I'm glad I'm being used in a good way for your needs."

She watched him disappear behind the hood and breathed a sigh of relief. If he had kissed her moments before, she probably would have fainted—or worse, burst out in emotional tears. She had to get a hold of herself. And it was as if he'd realized a kiss wouldn't have been a good move—she was certain he'd almost kissed her and thankfully pulled up. It had been the best action for him. And then he'd asked the right question, and she'd come clean to him about her past and the sadness hanging over her.

Even then, he'd been absolutely perfect. He had to be the kindest man she'd ever met.

CHAPTER FIVE

Austin led the way across town toward the auto supply business and continually looked into the rearview to make sure Tess was still behind him. She had been heartbroken when he'd found her inside her car, with her head leaning on her hand on the steering wheel. Seeing her like that, instantly, his hunch that she had something really bothering her had surged.

Her revelation about her parents' deaths broke his heart for her, but he had the feeling there was more. He could feel it twisting inside his gut, but he hadn't wanted to press her because her parents' tragic deaths were hard enough. The strain pressing over her was obvious, so he'd switched the conversation back to her car. But he planned to find out just how bad things were and how he could help her.

Because he was driven to help her.

He pulled into the parking lot, and she pulled in behind him and parked beside him at the end of the sidewalk. He hopped out and met her at the car door before she got out. "You can come in or wait here. Whatever you feel like doing."

She hesitated. "If you don't need me, then I'll just wait here."

"I'll be out as quick as possible." He headed inside and walked to the far wall holding the batteries. He grabbed his favorite brand and carried it to the counter. Moments later, he walked outside and after she lifted her car's hood again, he grabbed some tools out of his toolbox in the bed of his truck and went to work on changing the batteries out. Twenty minutes later, she had a new battery and the car started instantly.

"Thank you so much. I can't seem to stop having reasons to repeat those words to you. You are amazing."

Her words held sweet gratitude that twisted his insides once again. "You are very welcome. And don't forget, you are helping me out in a great way, uploading and organizing all those files. Seriously, we're helping each other." He gave her a pointed, serious stare because it was true.

Tess smiled gently. "Then, if you are serious about needing me to stay, my answer is yes. If your offer is still out there."

"Yes!" Excitement surged through him and he had to tamper it down. "The offer still stands. I'm relieved you're going to stay, and I don't have to look for someone else. Also, it's easy to tell that Ramona and Kimberly think you're perfect for the job."

Relief illuminated from her beautiful face. "That makes me feel good. I'll let my other boss know I'm not coming back."

"Sounds good. Is your wrist feeling okay right now?"

"It will be glad to get some more painkiller pumping around it, but it's doing better. Also, I'll be able to do more once my wrist is recovered."

"You're doing great. So, is there anything else I can do for you? Maybe buy you dinner?" He wanted her to agree to that but had a feeling she'd say no.

"Thanks, but you've done plenty for me today. I'm

going to let you head back to your ranch while I go put my arm on an ice pack. Don't forget to take this battery cost from my check."

"Fine, I'll do it, but I was glad to help. Rest well tonight, and call me if you need anything." He fought off the desire to hug her, to hold her against him and feel her heart beating against his wistful heart.

He watched as Tess got into her car. He shut the door then smiled at her as she backed from the parking space, lifted a hand in good-bye, and then drove toward her home.

Austin's heart continued its pounding against his ribs as he watched her disappear down the street. Then he smiled, realizing that she'd chosen to remain working for him instead of working late nights at weddings. He relaxed at that thought. He had time. Time to help her past the mourning she was obviously going through and anything else that might be bothering her. He liked her…felt a strong pull that it could be more considering he'd never felt this drawn toward someone. And maybe along the way, she'd agree to go out with him and let this budding attraction he felt have a chance to figure out whether there could be more between them.

He climbed into his truck and was about to head home to True Love when he got a text from his brother Cole, asking him to stop by before he went to his cabin. He had something important to discuss.

Important. The word had his interest, and he headed that way. As he drove down the road on the way back to the ranch, he passed the Harrison Ranch. It wasn't huge like their family ranch, but it was a nice, beautiful piece of property. Mr. Harrison had been friends with their grandfather and about two months ago, he'd moved to be near his son outside of Dallas. Since then, the ranch had just been sitting there. The older home to the side of the property drew Austin's gaze every time he passed it. The place was only about twelve miles from his office, and that wasn't as far as the nearly thirty miles his cabin on the ranch was. He'd been tossing around the idea of getting in touch with Mr. Harrison ever since he bought the practice from Dr. Perry. The house on it was hidden behind trees and would make a great place to start out in. But he pictured a new home, a family home in the center of the front pastureland at the top of the hill. He had been thinking about this every day he saw the property. Today, he knew he was going to call and find out if Mr. Harrison—Paul, to be exact—was interested in selling.

Twenty minutes later, he pulled up at the main house that Cole and Tulip lived in now since his parents had relocated to Florida. He exited the truck and strode toward the side patio of the stone home that he and his brothers had grown up in.

Cole pulled open the door and stepped out onto the patio about the time he stepped onto it. "Hey, Austin, glad to see you. Want some iced tea or hot coffee?"

Austin held his hand up. "Thanks, but I'm good right now. So, what's up?"

His brother gave him an arched brow. "Follow me to the office." He turned and headed back inside.

His reaction had raised Austin's curiosity as he followed Cole inside and closed the door. He trailed his older brother through the house. "Where's Tulip?" he asked as they entered the big office.

"She's over at Hanna's veterinary clinic, helping her plant some flowers and bushes. She loves what she does."

Tulip designed flower gardens professionally, so

helping her new sister-in-law with the outside of her clinic was probably something she was really enjoying. If Austin ever bought a house, he'd have to ask Tulip to help design the yard. He'd hire her but he had a feeling she would deny taking pay from him. But before he worried about that, first, he had to find a house.

His brother sank into his seat behind the desk, and Austin took one of the chairs facing him. "So, what is up? Is something wrong?"

"No, actually, I'm hoping something good is up. The Harrison Ranch has been offered to us for purchase."

Austin sat forward. "Seriously? That's the ranch I've been looking at every time I drive to Fredericksburg to the office. I've been thinking about calling him."

Cole grinned. "And I've been wanting to add it to the ranch's land. So are you in agreement that we buy it? We'll need someone to live out there, and you seem like the perfect one of us since it's halfway to your new office. Still interested? Or are you wanting to buy it as yours and not the ranch?"

"No, I think it's perfect to add to our ranch property

since I'll have little time to actually run the ranch part."

"Great. It has that small older ranch house hidden from view but when you get ready to build, you'll have plenty of great spots for a new house. If you want to build one." Cole smiled at him, as if he knew exactly what Austin would say.

"Yes, one day when I get married like you, I'll want to build."

"Perfect. I've already asked our brothers and they thought you'd be perfect for it also. Therefore, we're all in on this deal if you are."

"I'm in all the way and thrilled. I'll start in the small house and eventually, after I find a wife, we'll plan it together and build a house."

Cole chuckled. "You do know you've been taking care of your wife ever since Jake and Hanna's wedding? You caught that garter, then immediately raced over there and took care of that pretty Tess after she fell. And now, you've hired her."

The garter. Austin stared at his brother. He'd been trying not to think about the garter and Tess being connected. But there was no denying that he had strong feelings growing toward her and hadn't met her until she'd fallen down. "Do you really believe that garter stuff is true?"

"Yes. I caught a garter and the first woman I ran into was Tulip, and she needed me. Then Levi saw Rita first after catching the garter, and then Jake and Hanna. No it didn't happen that way for Bret and Ellie but still, it worked out wonderfully." He grinned widely. "But you caught Jake's garter and rescued Tess, so we've all been watching." He hiked a brow as he stared at Austin.

"You seriously believe that?"

"It's happened three out of four times us marrying the first woman we saw and four out of four time us marrying after catching the garter—so why wouldn't I believe it works? It's like we've had a great blessing delivered over us. And believe me when I say blessing. Tulip is the love of my life, and we're looking forward to the children we're going to have, hopefully soon. The other guys feel the same way. This is now your turn, and I think this spot is meant to be yours. It also gives us more cattle land and puts you closer to your office, your mission in life. And hopefully your future wife's future."

He stared at his older brother. It was all true, how all his brothers had fallen in love, but was it truly about the fact that Tess had been the first woman he'd encountered after he'd caught that garter? Yes, all of his brothers had met their wives right after catching a garter, but did that mean it was a real thing or a coincidence?

As much as he wanted to deny it, it had been tugging at him from the moment he helped her. The moment she'd looked up at him from the floor where she'd fallen, and instantly something inside him had shifted. And nothing had changed since. But he hadn't acknowledged the garter.

Cautiously, he met his older brother's eyes. "What you're saying could be true. I have strong feelings for Tess, and I just met her. But I'm not taking anything for granted. We shall see. But this opportunity to move to this ranch closer to my office is exactly what I want. I've been eyeing this place ever since he moved out but as you know, I'm not planning to raise my own cattle, so all of us owning the ranch is perfect."

"That's what I thought. So now, since you're in agreement, I'll get the deal moving forward—okay, actually, I already started the process. I was confident you were going to like it and if you didn't, the land was worth it anyway. But I didn't want you to think you had to take the house. It feels better knowing someone in the family is going to really enjoy it."

He grinned at his brother. Cole was an amazing head of the ranch. It was a spot he never wanted, and his parents had retired from running the ranch after they'd hit huge oil production. His other brothers were great at what they did to work with the cattle but, like him, they didn't want the top job, which Cole had been born to do. "Believe me, I will. My only question is, when can I move in?"

Cole grinned. "Two weeks. All the lawyers are busy on it. Mr. Harrison has his home cleared out, so the moment the papers are signed, you can move in."

He grinned. "Perfect. You, my big brother, read me perfectly."

"Perfect. How about your feelings for the beautiful Tess Piper?"

His heart skipped beats instantly. "We'll see. But I can tell you that I am drawn to her. That's all I know at the moment."

CHAPTER SIX

By the end of the week, her wrist was almost healed, not totally but far better than it had been, and this made Tess happy. She'd relaxed, knowing she now had a good job that paid more than her previous job, and she loved the two women she worked with in the office. And the doctor…she really liked Austin.

Something, other than he was a wonderful doctor and a great man, sent her heart thundering more every day she was around him. Or just thought of him, like now. But she had to be careful, not to assume anything. She just needed to continue on the path to get her life back on track and carry her parents in her heart, greatly loved and never forgotten.

"I'll see you next week," Ramona said, coming back from locking the front door. "I just want you to know I've enjoyed every moment working with you this week. I hope you have a great weekend and that your wrist is even further along on Monday than it is right now."

"Thank you so much, Ramona. It thrills me to be working with you and Kimberly. Before she left earlier, Kimberly also told me she really enjoyed our first week. I love it here, working with both of you. And my wrist is healing faster than Dr. Tanner thought it would. He looked at it this morning and all the swelling is gone. Though it is still hurting a little bit, it's so much better. He almost left the wrap off but told me he was afraid I'd overwork it if he did, so he kept it wrapped up." She grinned, thinking about his action.

"He's a smart doc, that is for sure. Have a great weekend, and I'll see you on Monday morning."

And then it was just Tess and Austin left in the building. She put her attention on finishing the file she'd been working on, getting the last pages loaded onto the copy machine, and copied it onto the computer file. That one done, she stood and grabbed her purse. She turned off the light of the front office, which had just been left on for her, and then walked down the hall. She was about to pass the closed door of Austin's office when it opened up and he stepped into the hall, and halted abruptly before running into her.

But she was so startled that she wobbled, and he grabbed her upper arms. "Tess, I almost ran you over. Are you all right?"

Electric shivers raced through Tess. "I'm fine. With the door closed, I thought you were busy, so I was heading out."

His fingers gently squeezed her arms before letting go. "I was going over papers earlier and about to head out to look at the new ranch we bought." He started walking toward the door and opened it, holding it open for her. Then he followed her outside. He quickly closed it, locked it and turned toward her.

Tess had frozen in place, startled by Austin's statement. "Y'all bought a new ranch?"

"Yes, me and my brothers bought a new ranch for more cattle. But it happens to be between here and True Love, and I'm going to live in the ranch house. I'd been thinking about calling the owner who'd moved away to be closer to his family. He was friends with us; my granddad had been a real close friend. Before I could call him and ask if he intended to sell it, he called Cole and ask him if we were interested. He wanted to give us first option since we were practically family."

"That's sweet. He must really be close to all of you."

"Yes, he is. Cole called me and asked me to stop by and I did. He asked me what I thought about the place, and if I'd like to live there. Turned out he'd already run the idea of me living there by our other brothers, and they were all in favor that it was a perfect place for me. It got me closer to the office but is still in the country. I've got some good brothers." He smiled widely, clearly meaning his words.

"That's wonderful," she said and meant it wholeheartedly.

"So, what are you doing for dinner? Why don't you ride out with me, and we can have a look, then grab something in town when I bring you home? It's Friday night and the outdoor restaurant in Fredericksburg has great food and music. What do you say?"

Her heart had practically stopped beating at his invitation. She managed to get a breath in, so she didn't have to worry about fainting in front of Austin. "You've really got my curiosity engaged, so I'd love to have a look. And you don't have to take me to dinner—"

"I don't have to," he said, cutting in. "But I want to. So, let's drop your car off at your place, and then you can get in my truck and we'll head out."

They did almost exactly that. But even though she was tall enough to get in the truck alone, even with a hurt wrist, he held her elbow and gave her a little help. Her elbow tingled even minutes later as they headed toward True Love—*the town, not the feelings in her heart.*

The thought kicked in hard. She barely knew him, and this unexpected brain switch of words was getting her carried away.

"The house is only about twelve miles from here."

"That's a nice, short drive in for you. But still gives you the ranch feel, which I have a feeling you love."

"Exactly." He smiled at her. "There's the entrance."

She stared at the entrance gate with the Harrison

Ranch sign and realized it would have a different sign. "Your ranch is the Tanner Ranch, isn't it?"

"Yes. Not sure if we'll put a sign up here. I'll leave that up to my rancher brothers. I'm the doc who lives on a ranch and tends to my herd at the office." He grinned, and she did too.

"You are feeling quite spunky tonight."

"Yes, I am."

It was obvious he loved the idea of moving here, and she totally understood it all. He pulled into the drive and headed down the gravel road. On the right, the road turned into two and he took the one heading to the right.

"The ranch house is there in the trees."

Tess saw it and was startled by the age of it. It was probably forty years old. Pretty but old. She'd expected him to be buying something newer. "It's pretty."

Austin pulled the truck to a halt. "Yes, it is, and it has a lot of family history. It's great for me right now, but later, when I marry, I'll be building a ranch house where that straight part of the road tops the hill. I'll show you the view. It's awesome."

He was waiting to build when he had a wife to build

it with him. The thought sent warmth radiating through her as their eyes locked. "That's wonderful. Already makes this a great place for you."

"I think so too. Now, let's go look inside."

* * *

Austin took the key and opened the door. "The sale goes through middle of next week, but I've been given the okay to start getting ready to move in. I'm not going to sleep here until the night after the papers are signed."

She walked past him into the house. "But I bet you'll have things you'll need moved in."

He laughed as he pulled the door shut. "You got that exactly right. It will feel weird at first not to live on the actual ranch, but the day after I move in, they'll be dropping off cattle, and unloading them into the pastures."

"And you'll feel more like you're on the ranch with Tanner Ranch cattle grazing around you."

His gut tightened into a ball as her lips curled in a soft smile, and he wanted more than anything to kiss her.

Her eyes suddenly widened, and she stepped back, as if she'd read his mind.

"Show me the house." She spun away and walked into the living room.

He followed her and knew he was in trouble and had to get her comfortable with him or she might run. Something had happened to cause pain to shine in her eyes at times, and his instinct told him it had nothing to do with her sprained wrist or the death of her parents. *What else had happened to her?*

"This is the living room, not huge but big enough for me and a few family or friends to spend time." The large fireplace was pale and dark stone, with a thick wooden mantel. He walked to the doorway. "The kitchen and dining area are here. One thing I might do is have this doorway widened or the wall removed. I'm not much on feeling closed in."

"Me either." She followed him into the kitchen. "In that little place I'm in, it is very closed in. After I've worked for you long enough to save up a bit, I'll probably look for something with a little more space." She smiled. "It won't be this big, but it will be a bit bigger and not falling down.”

“If I see anything I think you might like, I’ll let you know.”

“Thanks, but it won’t be anytime soon. But at least I have it on my dream list now.” She ran her fingers on the tile counter. “This is really nice. I guess even as old as the house is, they updated it.”

“About eight years ago. They did a great job.”

They walked down the hall, where there was a bathroom and two bedrooms. The last bedroom was on the other end of the hall and had its own bathroom. “I’ll assume this will be your room.”

He grinned. “You are very smart. Yes, this bigger room with its own bath has my name on it. My new bed will be arriving here tomorrow afternoon. I can’t wait.”

Tess burst into laughter at his obvious excitement about moving out here but what she didn’t obviously see was his excitement right now was having her here. Her gaze locked with his and his heart pounded harder thinking of her here sharing his house, his bedroom, his world with him. As if sensing his thoughts she stopped laughing, spun around and headed toward the door.

"It's time to see the back porch," she called over her shoulder as if it was past time for fresh air.

He agreed and followed Tess onto the back porch. He forced his mind to get right and to not think about the two of them in that bedroom. But in truth, it was a hard thought to push away. Ever since they'd stepped onto this property, his mind had been stumbling over thoughts of them as a couple. *Was she thinking the same things?*

"Are you ready for some dinner?"

"Are you sure?" Tess asked, not looking sure herself.

She was acting nervous, and he didn't want her to back out. "I'm certain. You deserve a really good meal in a fun place. I've already booked a table. So, the lake will have to wait another day for you to see."

"I'll look forward to it."

Austin helped her into the truck and made himself concentrate on helping her. They would have a relaxing evening, and he would suppress his desire to kiss her. Something that was getting harder and harder not to concentrate on.

They talked about the house the short distance to town, and he asked her for her opinion on curtains and rugs and even furniture. He had never decorated a house before. The small guest cabin he lived in had been furnished, something his parents had done years earlier for guests who came to the ranch. Now decorating this house would be his doing…and he wanted a place people could feel good about.

Fredericksburg was a busy place on Friday evening, so he parked in the first empty space he found, then went around and opened Tess's door. Her wrist was almost well but he'd encouraged her to give it some more time. He was happy that tonight he got to help.

"This is a very interesting town," she said as they stepped onto the sidewalk.

"Yes, it is. Texans and people from all over come to spend a little time here relaxing, shopping and dining. And then there are the ones who live here and love it."

They were walking down the sidewalk, past stores, as she smiled up at him. "How about you, do you love it?"

"Here we are." They had just reached a two-story

house with tables in the yard beneath thick trees. A man sat on the porch, playing his guitar and singing a soft love song. He didn't come here often but enjoyed lunch here sometimes. "I'll answer your question in a moment." There was a line of people waiting, so he stepped up to give them his name, which he knew was on the reservation list, and he hoped the table was ready.

"You have a reservation and your table is ready. Please follow me."

He held his arm out to indicate Tess go ahead of him as the host led the way to the last table on the left side of the band. He held one of the two chairs for Tess as she took a seat, and then he took his. The host told them the waitress would be by soon and then she left.

"You made a reservation? And we got seated before that line of people." She looked shocked.

He smiled, liking that he'd surprised her like that. "I certainly did. It's not a fancy place but it's a great place, with a lot of people wanting to get a table and listen to the music and enjoy the food. I didn't want you to have to wait in that long line, and I wanted to sit at this particular table and listen to the singer and be where we could talk comfortably. Not over there on the sidewalk." He touched her hand that rested on the table. "I hope that's okay with you?"

She nodded. "It is. I just wasn't expecting it. You thought of everything."

He'd tried. The waitress came, handed them each a menu, then took their drink orders and left them alone. Their chairs were situated closer on one side of the table, giving them both a view of the singer and giving them a closer sitting situation that he liked very much. There were booths inside the restaurant, but he'd thought she'd enjoy it outside, so this was great.

"So do you love it here in Fredericksburg?" she asked her question that she'd asked when they were walking up to the restaurant and he hadn't answered. She seemed very curious.

"I do, but it's not home. I love the ranch Mom and Dad raised us on, and I love the tiny town of True Love. It's a nice place but not really a place for a full-time doctor, therefore I had to make a decision to be here in this lovely town. But, it's close enough that many of the patients are from True Love, which makes me feel like

I didn't just run out on them."

"I'm sure they all understand. Who knows, after you have hired more doctors to work with you, you could open a once-a-week office there in your small town."

"You are reading my mind, I think."

She beamed. "I assumed you'd probably been tossing that idea around. It's just who you are."

And that was the amazing thing about her: she got him. "Thank you for those kind words. Now, let's study the menu so you can have a really good dinner."

"It definitely smells great. I can't wait."

CHAPTER SEVEN

On Saturday morning, Tess woke up feeling better than she'd felt in a very long time. And it had nothing to do with her wrist getting better. She'd had a wonderful evening with Austin, looking at his new home and then dinner. The music had been wonderful, and they'd enjoyed listening to it and visiting. Who was she kidding—she'd just enjoyed sitting so close to him and seeing the way he seemed to enjoy her being there beside him.

Yes, she should be cautious, but it was getting harder every day she was around Austin not to let her heart get involved. Something she'd sworn never to let happen again. Unable to just sit around today, she drove into town and parked her car across from the courthouse. She got out and began walking down the long street that had so many stores on both sides of the road that even if she chose not to enter a shop, because she had no extra money to spend, there was plenty of window-shopping she could do. One day she would have some extra cash again, and she had no plans to ever get tricked again. Because of her stupidity, she'd been unable to help her dad with anything other than being there for him. She had no money to even pay for his funeral, so thank goodness she'd been able to sell his truck.

Pushing the bad thoughts from her mind, she started walking and liking what she saw in the windows. She realized after she had been moving down the sidewalk for about thirty minutes that she was really enjoying herself. She paused as her heart caught at the thought…it had been a long while since she'd felt so peaceful. There was a bench where she'd paused, and she sat and let the reality sink in. Her life had turned a corner. And as odd as it sounded, it started after she fell at Jake and Hanna's wedding. The night she'd met Austin. She couldn't deny that meeting him had changed her life for the better.

Her phone rang, so she dug in her small purse. She had slipped the long strap over her head so the purse would rest on her hip. Austin's name shone across the screen and her heart instantly raced. She tapped the screen and put the phone to her ear and lips. "Hello."

"Hi. I hope you're having a good day. I had a great time with you yesterday."

A smile burst across her face. "I did too. And right now, I'm sitting on a bench in town, just enjoying being out and about."

"Good for you. Well, I called because my brother Cole and his wife Tulip have invited all the brothers and their wives over for an outside barbecue tonight. They stressed for me to bring you. They know you've come to work with me, and they'd love to see you since the last time was you hurting as I drove you away from the wedding. I'd love for you to come with me—had even thought about asking you before they requested that I bring you. I'll pick you up about six if you say yes. And I know I'm rattling on but I'm trying to convince you to say yes."

She was smiling hugely just from listening to him,

and now she laughed. "I would love to go with you. Your family seems really nice."

"Great. They are nice and so are you, so this will be a great evening."

She chuckled. "Great."

He laughed. "We're kind of short on words, aren't we?"

"That one works perfectly."

They both paused and she wondered whether he might be smiling as big as she was. "I'll be ready by six. What can I bring?"

"I'll be there to pick you up, and you only need to bring yourself. Believe me, there will be plenty of food there when all my sisters-in-law bring additions."

"And that's what I would love to do. Do they bring desserts, additional side dishes, dips…can you give me a hint?"

"Really, you don't need to bring anything. Just rest your wrist. They just want to see you and get to know you better, so yourself is all you need to bring."

He was trying to be nice, so she couldn't be mad. "Very well. I'll be ready when you arrive. I'm really looking forward to it."

"I am too. As is the rest of my family. See you soon." And then he hung up.

She breathed in deeply, feeling both excitement and hesitation about not taking something to add to the food list. But, if that was how they really felt, then she might upset them if she showed up with food. She stood and headed back toward her car. She was about to cross a street when she heard her name being called.

She turned and scanned the people on the sidewalk.

"Tess, over here."

Her gaze followed the sound to the side road. There was a woman who had been about to get into her car but now was waving at her. *Who was it?* Tess walked closer and then recognized one of the Tanner ladies. *Which one?* She'd not really been introduced to them at the wedding before she'd been hurt. She'd just been there to carry trays of appetizers. But they'd all looked really nice and pleasant. This one had beautiful cinnamon-toned hair.

"Hi," she said as she approached. "I'm sorry, I know you're one of the Tanner wives, but I can't remember which one."

The beautiful lady smiled and waved her hand. "It's okay. I'm Tulip Tanner, married to the oldest brother, Cole. I'm so glad to see you out and about. Has Austin called you about tonight?"

"Yes, just now." She smiled, really glad to meet Tulip. "I told him I would love to come for dinner and meet all of you."

"Perfect. Everyone will be excited. We were all so glad Austin was right there to help you. And extra excited to know you're working for him now. I had run to help Rita this morning at the office, and now I'm heading home. She just left, or I would introduce you to her."

Tess had heard that one of the ladies was a wedding planner and one was a yard designer, and another owned a florist shop, and they teamed up to put on weddings and other large parties. But that was all she'd known. She glanced over to where Tulip had waved her hand when she'd said she came in and worked, and it was a wedding planning shop.

"I heard a little about what you all do, and it sounds really great. I'll love meeting everyone. And yes, Austin has helped me hugely. I'm very appreciative."

Tulip's eyes scanned her face, as if trying to search her expression deeply.

Why?

"He is a great man and doctor. Okay, so I better get home and help Cole prepare for everyone. I can't wait to talk more. We are all wanting to make you feel welcomed to our area."

"Thank you for thinking of me, and I can't wait to visit more. Be safe. I'm headed home to get ready for Austin to pick me up."

"Great. See you soon." With that, Tulip got into her car, waved, and then backed out.

Tess waved back, then she crossed the street and headed to her car. Tulip had been super happy that Austin was bringing her to their dinner, and she had the feeling there was more to it than him fixing her arm and giving her a job.

* * *

Austin pulled up at Tess's and tried to shake off the feeling of happiness at picking Tess up and taking her to a family dinner party. He was a little nervous about the gathering because he knew what the whole group thought: that because he caught the garter at the wedding and then saw Tess, that she was his future bride. He was trying not to think of it like that, but he was growing crazier about her every time they were around each other. He hoped they didn't bring the garter thing up tonight. He'd told his brothers she didn't need that on her mind because she'd been through some tough time and was getting over mourning her parents. He didn't mention he was suspicious that something else plagued her also. The guys had promised they'd talk to their wives and make sure they kept quiet. Hopefully they all would not mention the garter because he didn't want her to think that was why he was trying to get to know her better.

He got out of the truck just as she opened the door. He stopped in his tracks, staring at her…she was beautiful. She wore a teal-blue sundress that flowed around her knees and exposed her beautiful legs and arms. "You are breathtaking." The words came out before he could stop them, and she blushed but thankfully didn't turn and go back inside.

"Thank you. I dug through my boxes of clothes that I hadn't unpacked yet and found this. I hope it's okay for the evening."

He smiled widely. "It's perfect." He walked around and opened the truck door as she locked her front door. Then he helped her in and noticed she smelled really nice. "I'm really glad you're joining me tonight at the ranch with my family. They are eager to see you again and actually get to know you."

"I feel the same way. I met Tulip in town earlier. She was so nice and told me how happy she was I was coming out with you. You have a great family."

"Yes, I do. And I have a feeling from how much you loved your mom and dad that you did too."

Her eyes softened instantly, and she smiled gently. "I really did. I loved them so much. Thank you for thinking of them."

Unable to stop himself, he lifted his palm and cupped the side of her face. "I can tell you they'd be proud of you and wishing you well."

"That is so very true. I'm sure your parents feel the

same way."

"They are. Mostly because they got to retire and not worry about anything." He chuckled, because it was so true. "I'll help you climb in and we'll get headed to the ranch."

Soon they were on the road, and he felt about as happy as he'd ever been. Something about this beautiful woman did that to him. And it wasn't as if he hadn't ever been around other gorgeous ladies…it was simply that there was something special about Tess.

And his family believed it was simply that she was the first woman he'd talked to after catching the garter. He felt like it was more than that.

CHAPTER EIGHT

"Fill me in on your brothers and their wives. Remind me of their names and who is with who." Tess looked over at her handsome driver.

Austin gave her a grin. "Okay, Cole is married to Tulip, the landscaper, and he is the head of our ranch. Levi is married to Rita, the photographer, and he is very active with the ranch business. Toby is Rita's son. And then there is Bret and Ellie, who loved each other long ago but Bret's professional rodeo career got in the way. Now, she's a florist and they're married and loving life. All of my brothers' love lives are very interesting, but that's basically all that matters anymore—they fell in love, and here we are. I'm still single and have a new career direction, and they are married and loving every moment. I'll be expecting baby announcements soon.

And then there is my youngest brother Jake and Hanna, the town veterinarian. They were the two who got married the other night when you got hurt."

"Yes, I remember them. You have a wonderful family, and I look forward to getting to know them tonight."

"You'll like them. My brothers each did well."

"It sounds like it." She wondered whether he would do as well. Her thought instantly went to her and him…but she shut that down. They were friends and he was her boss. She could be friends with his family, but she had had too much stolen from her this last year. Her parents both died, tearing her up inside, and before that nightmare had happened, she'd had the man she'd thought she was in love with steal everything she had, including her heart. Which was one reason she couldn't understand how she could so quickly feel drawn to Austin when she had been so betrayed, heartbroken, and emotionally destroyed.

She closed the door to those thoughts and focused on Austin's family gathering. It was going to be a great evening, and she was going to let herself enjoy it.

Moments later, they had driven down the long drive to the main ranch house. It was beautiful, older but gorgeous stone, and two stories. There were flowers everywhere. When they parked on the side between the large barns and the house, she saw the big patio, a pool, and a great view. "This is wonderful."

"Thanks. It's where I grew up, and we always did love it here. Tulip keeps this yard looking amazing."

"It is that."

"Okay, let's get over there. I see them coming out of the patio doors and heading this way. Let the fun begin." He grinned at her, and her heart nearly toppled out of her chest as she smiled back at him.

Within seconds after they climbed out of the truck, they were surrounded. Everyone was introducing themselves and smiling hugely at her as they did. She had never felt so welcomed in all of her life. They were almost acting as if she were part of the family who they hadn't seen in a while.

"We're glad you got to join us," Cole said. He looked at Austin and grinned. "You too. Come on, men. Let's go check on the brisket in the pit and let the ladies visit."

All the guys chuckled and followed their brother across the patio toward the large barbeque pit, where steam rose from the pipe on top.

"He's been cooking it for a long time today so it should be ready soon." Tulip started toward the house and everyone followed her.

Rita walked beside Tess. "We were so excited to hear you were coming tonight. We've been wanting to get to know you better ever since the wedding."

"We certainly have," Hanna said, looking over her shoulder at her as she walked through the patio door. "You and Austin had our attention that night—"

"But, we are so sorry you got hurt in your first encounter, though," Ellie interrupted Hanna.

Hanna reached out and touched her arm. "Yes, I'm sorry about that part. What I meant was we are glad you two met and you went to work for him. He needed you. Believe me, I'm a veterinarian, and I couldn't do without help. He was really in need and you saved him."

There was finally a pause and Tess smiled. "He has been a great help to me, so I was glad to help him. It was a great deal for me, accepting his offer. He's a wonderful doctor and his patients all love him. I'm thrilled to be in the office, helping. Now, what can I do in here to help all of you?" She felt the sudden need to get the conversation off her and Austin. They all seemed highly interested in them. And she was suddenly interested in them.

They gathered around the large kitchen island and began taking covers off potato salad, baked beans, and much more that all smelled delicious.

"All of you have gotten married over the last year, right?"

They all smiled at one another and then at her. Their eyes twinkled. It was as if they shared a secret or something, and she was suddenly extremely interested in their answers.

"Cole and I were first. He'd been at a wedding, caught the garter when it was thrown, and was coming home. I had been at my own wedding and was running away, and still wearing my wedding dress. My car hit a slick spot in the rain and ran off the road, and I barely had a memory when he found me walking down the road. We were destined to marry after he rescued me and helped me through some trying times."

"That is a wonderful story." She smiled, really having enjoyed the romance in the terrible situation. Her thoughts went to Austin briefly before she shut that dangerous idea down.

"I was a wedding crasher." Rita laughed. "Sneaking pictures at their wedding for a magazine. Levi saw me right before he caught the garter, and then he came after me. It was pretty much an adventure after that as he helped me and my little boy."

They had both mentioned the garters. "That sounds like an interesting meeting. Where is your little boy?"

"He's spending the night with one of his new friends, but you'll get to meet him soon."

"And you'll love that little boy immediately." Ellie smiled. "Now, my turn. Bret caught the garter at Rita and Levi's wedding, but oddly he didn't make contact with his bride-to-be that night, thank goodness. We had dated and broken up years ago and met again, not long after, though. I needed an interview from him, and my mom ended up needing help in her flower shop. In the end, after many complications, we couldn't deny our love and I'm so thankful. God is good. And now we gals join together to put on weddings."

Tess was relieved that the garter catching hadn't happened and she'd been the first woman Bret had seen. That was starting to get a bit worrisome, because she'd been the first woman Austin saw after catching Jake's garter. "That's really cool. Your story and the business you've all joined in."

She looked at Hanna, who was tossing a salad at the end of the island. "Okay, I have to hear your story."

Hanna chuckled. "I agreed to go to the town Christmas party and bid on one of the cowboys they were auctioning off. I never planned on bidding on Jake since we had dated briefly and I had turned him down after a couple of dates. So I had no intention of bidding on him…and then the bidding started and I couldn't stop myself. I kept bidding on him until he was the man who came and decorated my house for Christmas. And then the adventure of falling in love began and we married. Now, he didn't catch the garter that Bret tossed at his wedding, but he caught one thrown by a friend whose wedding we were both at, and then he ran into me. So, I can believe that the garter had something to do with it." She smiled. "It's a romantic thought, and I really think it did matter. It's a very dreamy idea. Don't you think?"

She realized all the women were watching her closely. "I think your stories are great."

"But what about the garter?" Rita asked.

"Oh, it makes it all more romantic." And it did. But knowing that it wasn't the lead-in for Bret and Ellie was a bit of a relief. Still, her thoughts went back to Austin catching that garter and then dropping it when he came immediately to help her when she fell. That garter catching was just a coincidence and a great tale for the ones who liked to believe in it. The fact that Austin caught the garter and immediately came to her aid was simply because he was a doctor. It was his natural instinct, and he was a quick responder. She tried to ignore the way he was looking at her when he caught the garter—and the way she felt in that moment before she fell.

Everyone was smiling at her, their eyes sparkling. "Why are y'all looking at me like that?"

"*Because*," Ellie drawled slowly. "Austin caught

the garter and was looking at you, then rescuing you. And they know the feeling, and even though mine and Bret's getting back together had a little different beginning, I can't help but look at the others and the garter story and think it means something."

"I agree," Tulip said, smiling excitedly.

"Me too," Hanna agreed.

"And I'll follow up with agreement with everyone," Rita finished what she'd started with her garter question. "You two look so good together. And you both look really attracted to each other."

She looked at this great group of ladies she'd wanted so much to meet and now, she felt a confusing ball of feelings. She liked them but at the same time wanted suddenly to run. "Are y'all expecting me and Austin to get married?"

Tulip's smile eased. "We are hoping the garter was a signal that love was about to develop between the two of you. Please don't take that the wrong way. We probably should have kept quiet, but we've been so excited."

She saw the concern in all of their eyes. They

thought they'd messed up and were worried. "Don't feel bad. Please. I actually really like Austin. But, well…to be honest, just a little before the month that I've been here, I lost my parents due to a car accident. And a couple of months before that, I went through a really bad dating situation. It's not a good time for me to be thinking about dating, much less falling in love and getting married."

Instantly, they each gave her a hug and said they were sorry about her parents and the bad dating situation. It suddenly hit her that she'd never told Austin about the lying creep who had stolen so much from her. Now that she'd mentioned it to his sisters-in-law, she might need to mention it to him. It was something she hadn't wanted to tell anyone about but now she had. And it was yet again another act of stupidity. Once she'd thought she was a smart person, but after letting that man con her, she would never fully respect her abilities again.

"We believe in you, Tess," Tulip said. "And we are here for you if you need us. But we also see the way Austin looks since meeting you. Something has changed in his eyes and we like it. So do his brothers. Therefore, we are rooting for you two to fall in love. But we will still be your new friends even if it doesn't happen."

"So true," Hanna said. "Now, let's get off this subject so you can relax and not feel like you are balancing on a thin rope."

Everyone agreed and that made her relax because she believed them. And the next little while, outside eating with the fellas, was wonderful. She had to admit that if there was ever a family she'd like to join, it was the Tanner family…but she wasn't sure she could ever trust her heart to anyone. And she wasn't sure, despite what her new girlfriends believed, that he would ever feel like she was the woman for him.

But despite all her thoughts, when he looked at her, her pulse pounded with hope and she had to try hard to ignore the wonderful feeling.

CHAPTER NINE

They had a wonderful time. His brothers had told him she was a great catch, and he'd told them to mind their own business. They just laughed at him, but he knew they would because they'd just been telling him that because of the garter catching tale. Even though he knew three of them had caught a garter and immediately met their future bride, that wasn't how Bret met Ellie. Oh, he caught one but didn't meet her until later, so that was a kink to all their belief that just because he caught the garter then helped Tess that they were destined for each other. And he was trying hard not to take their experiences and take beautiful Tess's friendship for granted as his future bride. She had been through a lot and though he found himself being drawn to her in a way he'd never felt about another woman, and actually started to wish catching the garter meant they were meant for each other, he wouldn't let himself believe that. He needed mostly to be her friend and find out what he suspected was haunting her.

Now, as he drove her home in the dark, they talked about what a fun night it was. That was a relief to him, that she thought that way. "I'm glad you enjoyed it. I did, and I know they did. You made a great guest."

"Thank you. But you are really blessed with such a close and wonderful family. My mom and dad were wonderful also, but I had no siblings, and all of yours make me wish I had had some."

"Yeah, I've always felt blessed." It was true. They were quiet for the last miles, him sad that he couldn't let himself kiss her, no matter how much he wanted to do just that.

When he pulled the truck to a halt, she removed her seat belt then turned toward him. His chest tightened and all he wanted to do was reach for her.

"Austin, I need to talk to you before I go inside."

He froze at the sound of her voice. "Sure. Is something wrong?"

She moistened her lips. "The girls revealed to me the wonderful ways they met your brothers. Three talking about being the first person each of your brothers saw after catching the garter. Ellie, despite not having met Bret that way, she was so excited about everyone else being the first person the other brothers spotted after catching the garter. It is romantic, even I have to admit it."

He needed to break into her words, but he couldn't. He needed to hear what she was thinking.

She moistened her trembling lips. "I know I was the first person you saw when you caught that garter. I hope you aren't thinking—or worse, hoping—that happens to us. No, let me continue," she said when he started to speak. "See, before I moved home to live with Mom and Dad, right before they were killed, I was dating this man. He seemed very nice, and I quickly started falling for him after just a few dates and cooking in my kitchen for him. One night, I was running late at work and he had asked me for my extra house key so he could get in and fix dinner for me. I didn't hesitate because I thought he was a great guy. When I arrived home an hour late, I found out differently. We had used my desk computer once, and he saw how to get on. As ridiculous as it was of me, he saw that my most used passwords for business sites were saved and plugged in automatically. It's not like I told everyone that, but he was beside me and saw me getting onto my bank account to pay a bill. I never thought anything about it. But that night, when he wasn't there and I found my jewelry box empty of my few pieces of jewelry, one that he had given me, I was suddenly horrified as the memory of him seeing my computer information slammed into me. I instantly turned on my computer and saw my bank account was empty. Everything I had been earning had been in my savings account and my checking account, and he took it all. Not a huge amount but it was a nice savings that I was going to invest soon, and he knew it. Anyway, I found myself so upset and feeling so ridiculous for trusting him that I moved home. And told my poor parents how stupid I'd been. They were so kind and told me I'd get through it, and then they were killed. It took everything they owned to pay their hospital bills and not leave them owing anything. They were not rich people but proud that they could pay their bills. They had refinanced their home at some point so after I sold the house it wasn't a huge chunk of money left for me to use paying off the bills the insurance hadn't paid. I also sold everything I could sell from inside the home in a garage sale, and paying off everything I could."

"I'm so sorry," he said, even if she wanted him to remain silent.

"And then I got in my old car and started driving and ended up here."

He reached out and cupped her cheek when he wanted to pull her into his arms. "You've been through a lot with your parents both dying. From what it sounds like, they'd be proud that you made sure their debts were paid. But that piece of scum who stole your money—did they not catch him?"

"He disappeared, and from what they suspected, using fake identities to steal from women was a common occurrence to him. And he knew how to disappear."

"That infuriates me."

She took his hand. "Please understand, I didn't tell

you this to make you mad. I'm telling you so you'll understand why I'm so glad to be your friend, but truthfully fighting off any attraction I feel for you. You are an easy man for a lady to fall for, but I just can't let myself. After all I've been through, losing those I loved and being used by someone I was falling for, I'm not someone looking for love. Just friendship."

He knew in that moment that he was interested in far more than friendship, but pushing for it was not going to do anything but hurt her after what she'd been through. Or make her run away. And he completely didn't want that. He needed to just continue on being there for her.

He gently touched her arm. "I'm here for you. I care for you, but I won't pressure you. Instead, I'm here to help you get on with your life and overcome the sadness of losing your parents and the anger of this jerk. I'm your friend. Okay?"

She blinked hard and he saw dampness in her eyes as she nodded. "You are special. And one day someone will be blessed to have you fall in love with them. I had a great time. Goodnight." And then she opened her door and stepped out. "I can open it, so please don't get out."

He sat there, not wanting to push her in any way. "I'll see you Monday."

"Yes." And then she closed the door and let herself into her little house.

He loved her. There was no denying it now.

He loved her, and he wanted to hurt the guy who'd stolen so much from her, including her ability to trust her heart to love again.

CHAPTER TEN

On Monday morning, Tess was working at her desk, trying to do her job and not think about telling Austin she'd made a horrible mistake by pushing him away after the dinner at the ranch. But she would not let herself say that because she wasn't ready to let herself fall in love again and especially with Austin, whom she believed deserved someone better than her.

So she was working hard on files, and Ramona was working hard at the appointment desk with calls and arriving patients, so she had no time to ask her what was wrong. The lady was good at her job. She could just look at patients and know they were sick; she could look at Tess and know she was troubled.

Thankfully, Austin was hugely busy today and didn't even take time for lunch. But by the time the office cleared out, he strode into their area and leaned against Ramona's desk. Kimberly came in, carrying her purse, about to leave to pick up her daughter.

"Okay, ladies, it was a busy day. I just wanted to tell you thank you for working so hard. Tess, Ramona told me you helped answer the phone and make appointments, so thank you. All of you were great today. Now, since I'm getting moved into the new ranch closer to the office slightly sooner than I thought, I want to have a fishing party out there for all the patients and their families and you and your families. It will take a couple of weeks to get ready, but if y'all could mail out an invitation card to everyone this week, that would give them all a week's notice if they are up to coming out for a barbeque and fishing. What do you think?"

Tess was amazed by him. "It's a great idea. I'll have the computer print off address labels for them, and I know Ramona and Kimberly don't have the time, so I'll fix up your invitation and get your agreement on it before I mail them out. Does that work?"

"Yes." Ramona came over and gave her a hug. "You are a dream come true."

Tess hugged the woman who'd become her friend. "So are you."

"You'll do a great job," Kimberly said. "And believe me, Austin, we will be there but I have to go now. See y'all tomorrow."

"Hugs, and see you tomorrow," Tess called.

"Thanks for helping me today," Austin called out as Kimberly hurried down the hall and out the back door. "And thank you, Tess. I completely agree with them. You'll do a great job. I appreciate you doing this."

"Sure. I'm glad to do it. After all, I work for you." She smiled, glad she had a reason for making the offer to help, and that it wasn't just that she would do anything for the man. Even if she knew she needed to back away.

"You two make a great team." Ramona smiled as she stood and picked up her purse. "See y'all tomorrow."

They said goodbye to her, and then Austin looked at Tess. "Thanks for doing this."

She held his gaze. "That's what friends do for each other. Anything else you need, let me know and I'll help."

"I'll let you know. Now, go on home. You can work on this tomorrow."

That was a good excuse to get out of the room, away from him. She was trying hard to be his friend but her mind kept drifting to how handsome he was, how wonderful he was, and how much she wished she was brave enough to shoot for more.

* * *

Austin called Cole on the way home and told him about the party, and that he was calling them all to invite them and get their input on ideas to help people—even the kids—fish.

"That's a great idea. Your patients will love it," Cole said. "How about food? Do you have that planned? I'm sure Tulip, Rita, and Ellie would love to help. But you never know with Hanna and her emergency schedule what she can handle."

"You said exactly what I wanted to hear, because I was thinking of calling them. I'll pay their fee."

"I'm not getting into that part of it. Knowing them,

they'll want this to be a family deal, but that's between all of you. I'll enjoy helping kids fish."

Austin smiled into the phone. "Great. Just have Tulip call me. Talk to you later."

"Hey, hold on. I know you are barely in but are you enjoying it out there?"

"So far so good. I'm settling in but to be honest, it's weird not passing by the main house and being able to stop and talk."

"You're welcome any time. You'll just have to get busy dating seriously."

He frowned as he pulled onto his drive and headed toward the house. "I didn't think I was ready for that, but lately it's been on my mind."

"And does it have to do with Tess? You two were great together at dinner the other night."

"Honestly, it does, but she's not ready for that. She's been through her parents' death and another…" He paused, realizing this was probably something she wasn't spreading around.

"The bad dating situation?"

"How did you know about that?"

"She told the gals at the barbeque when they were all in the kitchen."

And just now told him? He tried not to let the thought dig into him, but it was hard. "The guy was a regular user, stealing her money and savings out of her bank account and leaving her with almost nothing." He was actually glad to have someone to talk to about it.

"He did what? Tulip said Tess told them she'd had a really bad dating situation. But you're saying the dude ripped her off?"

So she hadn't gone into detail. "Okay, so maybe she hadn't meant it getting out to everyone. I misunderstood what you meant. But yeah, the guy was dating her and then got into her account and stole it all. That's why she was living at her parents' place when they died. I hope you can keep that to yourself. She's kind of lost after all that happening and ended up here, I think, just because she was driving and trying to get away from all the pain she was in. I wouldn't want to give her more pain."

"I'll keep it to myself, if you're sure at least Tulip wouldn't be a good one to know so she might be able to help her."

"I don't want her to think I've given away her trust. I'm sorry."

"I get it. Maybe if they are around each other enough, she'll talk to the gals and they may at least be able to listen and offer encouragement."

"That might be a good idea. I'll tell her they are working on the menu and hopefully helping me set things up, and maybe she can help."

"Sounds good. Now, did they catch the guy?"

"No, he's still out there as far as I know. He's probably doing it to his latest soon-to-be victim. No telling how many women he's stolen from. I may start looking it up."

"Let me know if I can help."

"Thanks, I will. Okay, talk to you later."

He ended the call and climbed out of the truck, then shut the door. He stood there with Tess on his mind as he stared out over the pastures with cattle grazing. It was a peaceful view but there was nothing peaceful inside him. He needed patience and she needed time; he was going to give it to her while he did some research on this jerk who'd robbed her of her money and her trust.

He entered the house and walked to the room that was now his office. He sat and turned on his computer. She'd lived in Houston when she'd met the guy who'd scammed her, and that was the place to start looking for others who might have suffered the same scam.

CHAPTER ELEVEN

By the following week, they had the party figured out. Tess was impressed with how Austin's family had jumped in to help him find a way to give back to his new patients. She was really impressed by the family. His sister-in-law Tulip had called on Sunday to tell her that they, the girls, were in charge of lunch and refreshments. She wanted her opinion; they were going to work one afternoon, if she wanted to come out and help them. And so she had, and thoroughly enjoyed her time with all the gals.

When she returned to work this morning, she had been trying to keep her mind on Austin just as a friend, but the truth was, she wasn't just crazy about him—now she was crazy about his family. When her eyes met with Austin's right after she arrived, once again, she wanted to tell him that she had made a horrible mistake pushing him away. But she wouldn't let herself.

"Good morning," he said. "Do you have a minute?"

"You're my boss, so of course I do." She gave him a small smile and told her pulse to stop going crazy.

Austin stepped into his office and she followed. To her surprise, he closed the door—she instantly froze in the middle of the room. *What did he want a private talk about?*

"Please have a seat." He motioned toward the chair as he went around the desk and took his chair. "I really appreciate how you are helping me with the gathering this coming weekend."

"I already told you I'm glad to do it. Especially after all you've done to help me. Do you need me to do something else?" The look on his face was serious. "Is something wrong?"

"No. Well, okay, I looked into your money being stolen from you."

His words stunned her. "Why?" she gasped.

"Because I care about you, and he took advantage of you. And it happens to a lot of women. I found a lot of information on numerous men taking advantage of women online on the dating sites. Is that where you met this guy?"

"No. Why did you do this?" She stood up, her stomach rolling. "I feel stupid enough about this. I have no idea why I said anything about it to y'all. It just came out while I was talking to the girls and then I had to tell you before they did. It wasn't so you'd start digging into it." She was shaking, she was so upset.

He was at her side instantly. He gently grabbed her shoulders. "Tess, I didn't mean to upset you. I'm trying to help you."

She blinked hard, trying not to cry. "I'm trying to forget it. I shouldn't have said anything about it to anyone. And now you're meddling."

His hands tightened reassuringly. "Only because I want to help you and to make sure you're safe. If this guy would do this, who knows what else he might do? You need to trust me and let me help."

Tess hadn't thought of that. She'd been totally startled by his stealing all her money he could get to through her online bank accounts. Looking at Austin, she knew he was a wonderful man. But trusting him as a boss and friend was different than letting herself ever trust her heart to love a man. *But he's trying to help you.* The words echoed through her, and she calmed down a bit.

She took a deep breath and let it out slowly as her thoughts churned. "I trust you. This was just so stupid on my part to have trusted him. You're different. You've been so good to me that it would be horrible if I didn't trust you. He had been great to me but he'd kept his past to himself, saying he'd had a horrible upbringing and had managed to leave it behind and that meant not sharing it with anyone. It made me feel bad for him, but it also made me want to be there for him. He'd recently lost his job when the company he worked for closed up and he had money, or so he told me, so he was looking for just the right job."

"And how did you meet him?"

"He was at a company meeting for customers. He'd come even though his company had recently closed." She looked away. "I learned later that he hadn't really worked for that company but had used it as a way to meet me. I think he had been watching me and must have thought I'd be a good target. And somehow knew I had savings that he could eventually get to if we were dating. Don't ask me how he knew this, but I have gone over it and over it, and that's what I come up with every time." Pain kicked through her at the thought of how planned out his plan had been to invade her life and savings.

"You're probably right."

"And I read a lot about other cases and realized that I would probably never get my money back. And when I did talk to the cops, they told me showing Nick my account wasn't a good idea. And I knew that but he arrived that one night and I was paying bills and he saw my bank's name and probably realized my password was saved to my computer."

There was a knock on the door. "Doctor," Kimberly said. "Your first patient is here. I've gone over her file and told her you'd be in next. Thought I'd let you know."

"Thank you. I'll be right there. Sorry," he said to her.

Tess stepped back out of his hold on her shoulder. "I'll get to work, too."

"Tess, please, can we continue this conversation later?"

"Sure, but I still think there's no use in looking for him. Talk to you later." She turned and let herself out the door. She wasn't sure now whether to be mad that he was digging into her past to try to protect her, or to be thankful for it.

She hurried down the hall and into the front office, trying to get her head focused on her work and not Austin's words.

"Are you all right?" Ramona asked, turning away from her computer. "You look upset."

"I'm fine. Just…getting ready for the big day on Saturday." She was lying, and looking at the true concern in her friend's expression made her feel totally wrong.

"Stop worrying. You and that wonderful group of Tanner brides will pull this off and make Austin proud and his patients happy. You and Austin make a great team, I think. He rescued you at the wedding and helped you through the wrist injury, and we got a wonderful friend and helper out of the deal. You are awesome. This weekend will be amazing." The woman's eyes glinted with assurance.

"Thank you. I hope so."

Ramona hitched a brow. "And maybe you two will have a good time, too, pulling it off." She smiled and turned back to open the window and greet a patient.

Tess turned away and sank into her chair. *Were her feelings for Austin so apparent?* If so, Ramona looked absolutely thrilled about it.

She left the office early, claiming she had to check on a few things for the party. It was true but she didn't really have to leave early; she just wanted to leave before Austin could talk more about Nick, the man she wished she never had to think about again. She just wanted to forget him and pretend she'd never let herself be swindled.

* * *

Austin drove into Tess's driveway but saw her car

wasn't there. She had cut out from work early to avoid him, he was certain. And now, knowing this was where he would come, she was continuing to avoid him. *Was he overstepping his position?* She wanted nothing to do with finding the scum again. That really bothered him. Shouldn't she want to put him in jail—prison—for what he'd done? He had a feeling the man had done it to others, like the men he'd read articles about. That one creep had taken a huge amount of women to the poorhouse before he'd finally been caught. And that had only been because several of the women had helped catch him. But he also knew doing that had stolen time away from them moving on with their lives. So, had he been wrong, trying to get Tess to let him hunt this man down?

He had money. His family's huge ranch had hit it big on oil; he hadn't even had to make money being a doctor, but it was what he wanted to do with his life. But if she really refused to have anything to do with having this dude hunted down, then she'd hold it against him. He was in a tight spot. He wanted to do whatever he needed to have Tess fall in love with him, because he loved her so much. He'd admitted it to himself and there was no going back.

He drove out of the driveway and headed toward home. He had to think about this. Maybe talk to his brothers. But that might be putting too much pressure on them, adding more reasons for Tess not to let him deeper into her life.

The last thing he was expecting was his brothers unloading logs that would become the marshmallow-melting campfires for the families. And it looked as if they had unloaded long, thick logs for seats around the campfires. He parked, got out, and headed their way, more than glad to have something distract him from his troubles.

"Just in time," Bret called. "Is it looking like you want it to?"

"It looks great. I had no idea y'all were bringing it out today."

Cole came over and placed his hand on Austin's shoulder. "We knew you had sick folks to take care of, so we didn't bother you about it."

"That's right," Levi agreed. "We figured we'd still

be here about the time you arrived, and we could make sure we have it where you want it."

Levi placed the two fire logs he was still holding on the fire stack. "So what do you think about the places we have them?"

He looked from one fire stack to the others. "They're great. Close but not too close, and it leaves that area to the left open in case anyone wants to kick balls around, and then the lake for fishing. And horse riding in the ring. Did you hire some of your men to take that position for the night?" He looked at Cole.

"Yes, some of my calmest men will be running that part of the night and looking out for the kiddos."

"Sounds great. My patients got their invitations and are looking forward to coming out."

"Great," Cole said. "I'm glad to be involved in this, and it's perfect for this new ranch. And for you. The gals are excited too. Tulip said they are all enjoying planning this with Tess. They're all shopping tonight, getting decorations and party items they know kids will enjoy, like bubbles and treats, and they're eating together before they come home."

So that was where she was. "They have all been great to help out. And I'm glad they get along with Tess like they do."

Jake grinned. "How do *you* get along with her?"

Eyes from all of them drilled into him. "I like her a lot. But she's gone through a lot, and I just can't push her toward a romance when she's still getting over losing both of her parents."

"You're there for her." Levi's eyes softened. "I totally understand that, because I'll never forget stepping in to help Rita make it through starting life back. You're doing good. Hang in there."

Levi's words struck deep in his heart. "I really needed those words," Austin said with a sigh.

"Move slow, and it will happen when the time is right," Cole said. "Okay, fellows, let's get back to our homes. Call if you need anything."

Austin watched them load up into the two trucks they'd come in. He waved as they drove away, and then he climbed into his truck and drove the short distance to his house. The area was so spread out that he'd rented an outdoor trailer restroom that had a men's side and a ladies, and the guests wouldn't have to walk the distance from the lake to the house to relieve themselves. It was arriving on Friday morning, as were the tables and chairs and the tent to give everyone a relief from the sun if it was just too hot for them. By the time he parked at the house, he'd run through everything. He thought they were prepared. It should be a fun day.

As he walked into his house, he tried to keep his focus on the positive thoughts about the party. But as he filled a glass with ice and then water, his thoughts were on Tess. He wondered how she was doing through all of it since he'd shaken her emotions with the stuff about her past.

This was supposed to be a great weekend, and now he wasn't confident in how he and Tess would handle it when he'd put this roadblock between them.

CHAPTER TWELVE

By Saturday morning, everything was ready for the party day. Tess and Austin's family all arrived early to make sure everything was in place. It looked great.

"Your patients are going to have a great time," she said, as they all gathered in a group before they started to arrive.

He smiled and looked around the group. "That's thanks to you and everyone standing here. I need and want to thank you all for what you've done. And what you're planning to do today to help my patients all have fun. It's almost like this is my official party for me and my new beginning as a community doctor. A man who gets to know my patients and their families as I help them with my treatments."

"We always knew you'd be a great doctor," Bret said. "I can still remember when we were young and started riding on the back of larger calves. If we fell off our bucking calf, you came running to make sure we could get up and that we were okay."

Tess watched with pleasure as all of his brothers added things to the remembrance of Austin's journey to knowing he was meant to be a doctor. She planned to tell him later, maybe after the day was ending, that yes, he was meant to be a doctor, not an investigator who tried to find a swindling man who conned her and probably many more. His job was to help sick people get well, not correct her mistake that she was determined to move past with a big lesson learned. That had been one of the last things her dad had said to her before he died. And she planned to listen to him.

She had dug out some denim jeans shorts she had and a red tank top for the day. And a pair of white tennis shoes that would not last long if she got too close to the muddy area of the lake. She would leave that area up to Austin and his brothers, and the kids and their families. She would stay by the refreshments and the ball games anyone might want to play.

Cars started driving up at that moment, enabling her to keep her distance for now. But then he called out her name and she turned back to see what he needed. He was walking toward her with intent. When their eyes met, he smiled, sending a shiver of yearning through her. She couldn't speak.

"Look." He stopped in front of her. "I want to thank you for all you've done, and I need to tell you I'm sorry I pried into your past. Please don't hold that against me."

"Do you really mean that?"

"Yes, it's your call. I stepped over the line and expected you to do what I thought was right. It took me all week to finally understand only you can decide what you want out of a situation. So, I just wanted to tell you that before we got busy today."

Her heart pounded. She stepped forward and slid her arms around his waist. "Thank you." Instantly, she stepped back. "Now, have a great day. I'm going to enjoy playing with the kids."

"Thank you. Maybe we'll run into each other as the

day moves along." He grinned.

"Maybe," she agreed and then swept away and hurried toward the refreshment area to help. "This might be a great day after all," she said softly to herself and her smile broadened automatically.

Tess made it to the food section, smiling at everything that they had decided to have for the kids. There were cupcakes, a variety of cookies, and a lot of watermelon ready to eat. She had a feeling that Austin hadn't taken any shortcuts, and everything was as healthily made as possible. She got behind the table and made sure all the plates and forks were out, and she saw that Rita was doing the same thing over at the drink table. This was morning snack time—it was about ten o'clock by now—and lunch would be later, although she kept looking at this table full of delicious-looking treats and wondered whether any of the children would be interested in lunch when it showed up.

"This all really looks good," she called to Rita.

"Tell me about it. I am craving those cupcakes."

"Well, believe me, there's extra boxes under the table, so I think there will be plenty."

"I hope this beautiful sunshine doesn't melt all the icing."

"They are in an ice chest to keep them frosted." She smiled as Rita immediately came over and helped herself to a silky vanilla cupcake with sky-blue icing, topped with a mini marshmallow.

"This looks like a beautiful sky on a sunny day." She took a bite.

"That's exactly what they called it the day I picked it out. You're good."

"No, you are, because you knew what would appeal to kids and adults."

"I really wasn't sure, so you just made me happy." Tess really hadn't been sure but now felt better about it. All the Tanner wives had chosen lunch items, hamburgers and hot dogs they were sure everyone would love.

Rita's expression grew serious. "Is Austin making you happy? I mean, are y'all dating yet? Or are you still fighting the romance building between you?"

"It's not that easy."

"I can tell there is something between the two of

you. We can all tell it, but something is stopping you. You haven't shared it with us, which is your option. But when I met Levi, I was in a very hard position also. I could have walked away, but he made an offer that I couldn't refuse and with his help, my life worked out." She smiled and nodded toward her husband Levi, who was playing with her son, Toby. "And so did my little boy's. So, I'm just hoping you won't deny this time with Austin. If you love him, and I feel like you do, then give this life with him a chance." She reached out and gently pressed Tess's forearm. "And I'm here if you need me."

Tess watched her walk toward her family and join in on getting the fishing poles ready. Her heart squeezed tightly with the sweet family picture they presented. She had wanted exactly that in her own life and was afraid to ever open up to that again.

Tess walked away from the dessert table because everything was set up so people could help themselves, therefore she didn't have to be there all the time. She watched Austin as he waited for all of his patients to park on the mowed grass. The kids would run ahead of their parents and throw themselves at him and then begin asking him questions—at least, that was what she assumed they were doing as they pointed at the lake. He was all smiles as he answered their questions and greeted the parents, then pointed at the various areas of food, games, and fishing. Then the family would head toward where his brothers were handing out fishing poles. And he would greet the next family the same way, with smiles and hugs and directions. It was obvious he was enjoying himself.

She was certain he had been an excellent emergency room doctor but this was what fit him. He was very good with all members of a family: kids, parents, and grandparents. He had a big mixture of patients who had come from the previous doctor, Dr. Perry, but they had stayed with Austin after meeting him. Ramona said that the doc had anticipated that his clients would like Austin and that they'd quickly know he was a great doctor. Ramona had smiled and said, "A great doctor replacing a great doctor." And Tess believed that Ramona knew exactly what she was talking about.

This was going to be a great day and she was so

glad she was here.

At least, for now. Just watching him from this distance, she knew she was going to have some major decisions to make.

* * *

"This has been a great day," Cole said as he reeled in the line of the little boy he was helping, while the dad helped the little sister reel her fish in.

Austin grinned. He stood beside his brother, enjoying the day. He had been helping another young man who had to leave early. They'd been thrilled about how the day had gone and hated to have to leave early. Austin was glad about their reaction to the family day and all the others who were attending. He planned to at least do one a year.

"I've really enjoyed it myself, and it looks like everyone is." Austin glanced over and saw a little kid reeling in a fish; his mother was going wild with excitement as the dad helped the happy boy get it out of the water. "Good example right there."

Cole grinned. "Yes, it is. It's been a great day for everyone. Including that hardworking, tremendously nice, accommodating Tess. She's been nonstop helping people get food, refreshments, played many games with kids. Whatever they needed, she hasn't stopped. All the gals have said she's been amazing."

Austin glanced back toward the refreshment tables and game area. He had been keeping her in his sight all day. And he owed her a huge thank-you. As he did all of his sisters-in-law and his brothers. They had all helped this be a successful day. But he felt like he owed Tess something super special. He hadn't really known how she would be today but she'd been amazing. He would have never guessed that she had any sadness behind her eyes or in her heart for her parents. Or any troublesome emotions from that creep who had stolen all of her money. The creep he'd been struggling to push out of his thoughts. She wanted nothing to do with finding the man and bring him to trial. She wanted to forget the guy existed and erase him from her past.

The truth was that the more he thought about it, the more he understood her thoughts. She didn't want being connected with that creep pulling her back into those memories. She probably, like so many of the victims of similar robberies, would never get her money back. A guy like that dated a woman until he was able to steal from her. Then he'd disappear, under new names and IDs and lots of lies.

"Are you going to let Tess get away from you?" Cole asked.

"It's not something that I can make a decision on. Yes, I love her but, she's been through a lot and she has to love me, and if she does, she has to love me enough to push the pain she's carrying away. And she has to trust her life with me in it. Anyway, I'm going to go get something to drink. Can I bring you anything?"

"No. If there is some beautiful lady you can have a conversation with, I don't want you having to halt it so you can bring me a drink. Go, and take your time. I'll talk to you later," Cole said with gentle urging. "I'm sure you'll get this figured out. Now go."

Austin took a deep breath, turned, and headed across the pasture. He hoped his brother was right.

She was straightening up the dessert table when he

got there. The desserts were almost gone and he had been pleased how well the "better for you" desserts had been received.

"You've done an amazing job today."

"Thank you." Tess smiled as she looked up at him. "Everyone has completely loved this party. And that's because you gave it to them."

"You and my sisters-in-law and my brothers helped put this success together. I doubt on my own I would have had anything near as great as what y'all came up with."

"Well, thank you. One of the many things I can say about you is that you do not mind sharing accomplishments with others."

"I would be a fool if I didn't do that."

Her smile widened. "There is nothing about you that would be considered a fool."

"You want to take a walk?" He sure hoped she did. She looked around and he did too. Everyone looked busy and fine.

"I would love to."

He headed down toward the lake but not to the lake;

instead, they walked in the mowed grass between the fishing group and the refreshment area. "So are you doing okay?"

"I am." She paused. "I'm really glad I came, because it has been fun."

"It's almost time for that two people tied together race that Hanna suggested. I was thinking you could race with me."

She stared at him, then smiled. "That would be fun. We just have to be careful and make sure I don't fall and break my wrist." She smiled and lifted her newly healed wrist.

He smiled back at her. "I promise you that if we fall, you'll land on me. I'll make sure of it, and your hands will be protected."

"Okay, that sounds like a very nice…well, that doesn't sound right, does it? That sounds like a good solution. But you can't break anything either. What would all these patients do?"

"They'd have to get used to my fill-in."

"You know, Austin, you are a great doctor and I can't even imagine how you haven't been a family doctor from the beginning."

He shrugged. "I thought about it in the very beginning. And I thought about it being this particular spot, helping out Doc Perry. But I was helping in the emergency room early on and was just hooked on it after that night. I helped save three people that night. It wasn't easy, but I couldn't leave after that and so I stayed there. Now, it's almost like Doc Perry knew it was time for me to come into his family practice. He knew it was time and he made me an offer I couldn't refuse. And I'm glad I'm there, and I'm glad you are too." He closed his eyes for a moment and hoped he hadn't said all the wrong things.

Thankfully, he hadn't accidently told her he was in love with her. He couldn't do that now and he knew it. That would completely run her off.

"Thank you. I'm glad I'm there too."

They'd stopped walking and stared at each other. He wanted more than anything to pull her into his arms, feel her body pressed against his, and to take her soft lips to his. But he didn't.

CHAPTER THIRTEEN

Everyone gathered together about thirty minutes after she and Austin had walked together. They all gathered in the open area where she had been playing kickball with the kids earlier. One of the older men, a patient and grandfather to one of the kids, was going to shoot the fake gun to get them started. She and Austin were now tied together.

He had wrapped the rope around their ankles and then he'd looked up at her and grinned as he stood. "Now I'm going to wrap my arm around your waist and you're going to wrap yours around mine, and then we are going to run as fast as we can to the finish line."

She laughed, totally enjoying this moment, despite knowing it was affecting her emotionally. "Okay. I hope we can run really fast because there are a lot of people who look like they are ready to beat the crowd." She glanced down the row at all of his brothers and their sweet wives. They were all grinning back at them, probably thinking the same thing, that they might get beat by the kiddos and their parents, but that they were going to beat their brothers and their partners.

"Oh yeah, me and my brothers were very competitive growing up. But there are a lot of people out here who look just as competitive. Although it's mostly dads and sons, or dads and daughters and some mothers who look just as determined to help their child win. There aren't that many moms and dads competing, therefore we have to be careful. We don't want to beat them."

She laughed. "You think that would be a good physician thing to do?"

"Well, I can't really figure it out. If I was able to manage a win, that might make them all feel good about me being their doctor, seeing how determined I am to make things happen. But I've got some really fast brothers out here, and if any of their wives happen to be fast too, hmmm, going to make it interesting. How fast are you? Are you going to put me to shame and drag me along with you?"

"Oh, you have nothing to worry about on me dragging you. I have a feeling you are going to lift me up with this muscled arm of yours and you'll carry me over the finish line. If you plan on winning."

"That's a pretty good idea. It'll give me a good excuse to hug you close and lift you up…well, maybe I need to shut up before I get myself in a bad spot."

They stared at each other and she had the biggest craving to get on her tiptoes and kiss him. She was in major, major trouble with that thought.

"Everyone, line up," the man with the megaphone called out.

"It's time for the race." Austin's arm tightened around her waist and his hand tugged her even closer so that her side was crushed to his side. "Are you ready?"

She looked back up at him. "Lead the way and I'll try hard to keep up."

The man called out, "Ready, set, go!"

And everyone in line tore out toward the finish line. Some, she noticed, were stumbling and falling; some were hopping and staggering. And she was laughing as they stumbled momentarily. Then Austin tightened his hand on her waist, lifted her feet off the ground, and began to travel quickly beside his brothers, who were doing basically the same thing. Then a dad and son running on the right of them stumbled and slammed into her side, causing Austin to stagger and they were falling toward the ground—her on the bottom side. But in a split second his arms engulfed her, his body forcefully twisted and, to her startled surprise, she landed on top of him. It was a hard, rough landing but like he'd promised, she'd landed on top. He'd kept the promise. The man was amazing.

"Are you okay?" he asked, his voice weak from all the pressure he'd endured.

"Fine, thanks to you. How are you?"

"Can't move at the moment but will be fine when I get a bit more air."

"Oh," she gasped. "Let me get off you so you can breath—"

His grasp tightened around her. "I'm perfectly fine." His gaze dropped to her mouth, drawing her head to drop slightly in hope for a kiss.

Cheering suddenly broke out, startling her. She yanked her head up, amazed at what she'd almost done. She saw that everyone was cheering for the winners of the race. "Let me get up." She didn't wait for him to protest but scrambled off him. But she couldn't stand because they were still connected, so she grabbed for the rope that tied their ankles together. He sat up and gently moved her hands out of the way as he took over. She looked at him and he smiled before looking down at the rope. Her insides shivered.

"Didn't mean to shake you up or upset you."

"I'm not upset. I just have to straighten out my thought process."

Their ankles were now released from the rope and he looked at her. "I just want you to know that I'm always here for you and I...care for you."

He had said "care" but she could see in his eyes that he felt more for her and she had to hold herself together. "I need to go help clean up, because this is the end of the day, right?"

He looked startled at her reaction. "Yeah, we're

going to wrap things up and believe me, nothing would have been as good as it was if you hadn't helped."

"Thank you for saying that. I enjoyed it." And then she got up and almost ran to get away.

* * *

They finished the afternoon, and Austin's brothers and their wives kept giving him glances as they helped the kids and parents prepare to leave. Finally, he waved goodbye to everyone and thanked them for coming out and for using him as their doctor. He was glad that he'd had the party for them but his mind was distracted over Tess, who was steadily cleaning up the tables. She had not come close to him since she'd fallen with him onto the ground and, he was certain, been tempted to kiss him. But then she'd wanted to get away from him. He had so wanted to kiss her and thought for a moment, while she'd been laying on top of him after he'd kept her from hitting the ground, she'd looked like she'd wanted to kiss him. But then as she'd hurried away to start cleaning up, she'd looked like she was running away. As fast as she could go, just to avoid them getting any closer.

She was so messed up from that man, the creep who had done her so wrong, stealing everything from her right before she lost her parents. His heart ached for her. The last thing he wanted was to be someone who added to her pain. But she had almost kissed him, so now he was even more torn than when the day had started.

Cole walked over. "We all decided to stand back earlier when we saw you and Tess rolling around on the ground during the race. We had hoped maybe something good would happen because of that interesting situation. But you have been very distracted since and haven't really looked happy. So what's bothering you?"

"She, well, you know I told you she had a fella rip her off. After this con man had stolen everything, you know, I was going to try to find the guy and see what we could do about putting him in jail. But when I told her what I was wanting to do, she didn't like it at all. She told me that she didn't think she'd ever get her money back and she wanted to forget it. Right after this happened, she'd moved home and lost her parents and was mourning their deaths. Her life had become pretty awful. She came here to try to start over. Then, at the wedding, she got hurt and I was able to help her. But she can't let herself be involved with me. She just wants to move on."

"Wow, it's very complicated, isn't it."

"Yeah, tell me about it. But you know, when you think about it like she does, he's probably used all her money and she'll get nothing back. It will just take up all her time, pay her nothing and just put her out there where people will know what happened to her. She just wants to forget it and start over. I feel bad that I dug in it at all and caused her more pain, because in all honesty, I'm furious with that guy. I'd like nothing more than to beat the…tar out of him and send him to prison. But I understand where she's at now, with the thought of this going live to everyone and her not just having a quiet starting over time like she's trying to have. She is very attracted to me, and I think she cares about me more than she's letting on. She even smiled at me before she walked away. But now, she won't even look at me. Now I'm worried that she will quit her job and leave town to avoid me getting any more involved in her past. I think I've really messed up."

"It's very complicated, and I feel for the position you're in. And honestly, after what you just said, I can't say that hunting the dude down and putting her in the limelight to have this linger over her for the rest of her life is the best thing. I can see how that would mean it could always haunt her and if he's used all her money, she'd get nothing back from it. Yes, it might save someone else from having it happen, but really, Austin, because she was dating the guy, that might stand against her on getting him arrested or convicted. I feel for you both. It's a tough situation. But, Austin, in all honesty, it's her decision. You can't take on her past of what happened by going after this guy if she doesn't want you to, because she's the one who will have to deal with it. Can you handle that?"

Austin raked his hand through his hair. His brother was speaking the truth that had been weaving through his own mind. "I was going to try, but it is tough. I want to bring the right stuff into her life, but that man owes her something. Yet you're right; it's not my place to override her choice. If I do anything more, I'll lose her."

"Yeah, so think about it differently. If you can win her over and marry her, like I'm pretty sure you are wanting to do, then you can protect her in case that creep shows back up in her life."

"That is a very good thought. And I am in love with her. There is nothing in this world that could ever make me as happy as being able to have Tess in my life."

Cole put his hand on his shoulder and squeezed. "Well, I can tell you, even though your other brothers and sisters-in-law don't know how deep and troublesome what's going on between you two is, I'm here for you and they are rooting for you."

Austin watched his brother turn and walk off. Then, deciding it was best to give Tess space, instead of going over to help her do what she was doing, he turned away. His sisters-in-law were headed her way, so she'd have plenty of help and wouldn't need him. Turning, he headed toward the fishing poles. He'd gather them up and put them in storage and at the same time, he pushed his heart into storage also.

CHAPTER FOURTEEN

"What is going on between you and the doc?" Ramona asked at the end of the following week. She had turned toward Tess the moment she'd closed the sliding window after taking the next patient's information.

"Why are you asking that?" Tess asked.

"Because all week, you two have barely spoken to each other." The older woman stared at Tess, as if daring her to deny what she'd said.

"Well, he's just been busy."

"Like I don't understand that he has been busy. But if he needs you to do anything, he asks me, when I go back to his office, to let you know. Instead of calling you back there and just asking you himself. I've been watching after the first half of the week, just to make sure I wasn't imagining things. And you can tell me I am as many times as you want to, but I know I'm not.

"Look, you two are very good together. I know we didn't get to talk much at the picnic the other day because I was busy with my little family, but I watched, and he kept watching you. Even when he was busy, he always seemed to look in your direction, keeping you in his sight. And you were doing the same thing. Believe me, I was sitting in a lawn chair by the lake and had a view of everything. My husband was busy with the grandkids, and so was their daddy and mama. I watched them playing and fishing, but I also watched the entertainment of you and Doc. You cannot deny the truth that you two are attracted to each other."

Ramona had leaned forward in the seat of her chair and was talking quieter so, Tess assumed, if the doctor came out into the hall, he couldn't hear her. At least Tess hoped so. "Ramona, I know you are only asking me these things because you care, but there is more going on in this situation than you know. My life has been rough these last several months and I'm very, very thankful to Austin for helping me in more ways than just fixing my sprained wrist. But I can't get my…well, there is something that happened in my past, and I can't completely move forward from it."

"I know you lost your parents, and I am so sorry for that. But why would you let that keep you from letting someone who I think loves you into your life? You've lost those who loved you and you loved, but now you could have more love in your saddened heart."

She looked around to make sure no one was listening, which made Tess appreciate her. Despite the intrusion into her personal life.

"It goes further than that. And, it has nothing to do with my sweet mom and dad. Look, you have someone coming up to the window, so can we just move on from this?"

"Okay, for now. But I have a fear you are going to mess this up. And personally, I think that would be a wrong move on your part. That is a wonderful man in there treating ill patients, and he cares for you. You two make a wonderful couple." She turned back to the window, opened it, and greeted the patient.

Tess turned back to her work, her heart pounding

and her stomach sick. *How was Austin actually feeling?* She had drawn back from him and had not missed his drawback from her. Both had pulled back after she had almost kissed him that day they'd been tied together and rolling on the ground in the pasture. After he'd released the rope tying them together and she had risen and walked away, she'd been slammed with the truth. *She loved him.*

Loved him desperately, and yet when she looked at his wonderful family, his amazing sisters-in-law, his great brothers and their family relationship, she knew she wasn't good enough. She didn't fit in. She'd been so stupid, losing everything to that horrible man she'd thought was an awesome man before he'd totally tricked her and stolen all her money and savings…she felt so small. The man had targeted her, she had decided. He'd hung around until she'd let her guard down. It was so embarrassing, and she didn't know whether she would ever get over it. Especially if others knew what had happened.

She had absolutely no confidence that she could help bring that man to trial. Nor did she want to live with exposing herself to everyone about how she'd trusted such a horrible man and then for others to know he'd just walked away. It was far too embarrassing that she'd fallen for his lies.

She'd read after that about other women who'd been through the same thing, and they also felt what she felt. But they took a step forward and exposed the man even though it didn't bring him to justice. *She just couldn't do that, could she?*

She had read so many articles and reports. Even though a few men were caught and prosecuted, more were not. She had hoped to just quietly leave it behind and eventually hope to start over when the right man came along.

He had arrived…but he was so wonderful and deserving of a smart, delightful woman in his life. And she didn't feel like that woman. Now what was she going to do?

* * *

Saturday morning, still struggling with what her next

move should be, Tess got dressed in jeans and a T-shirt. Then she got a cup of coffee and sat at the table to stare out the window and think. But she was feeling really distraught because her thinking was nothing more than thinking of Austin. And how bad she was going to feel if she did the only thing she believed was right, and that was leave town and tell no one where she'd gone.

She quickly took a drink of her hot coffee and let it burn its way down, trying hard to let it tell her this was what she needed to do. But could she?

Her phone rang. She glanced at it and saw it was Tulip. "Good morning," she answered, trying to make her voice sound normal.

"Good morning to you, too," Tulip said. "Me and the girls are taking a road trip to relax and we thought you might want to come along. We were actually hoping you would join us."

Going with the wonderful four new friends was a great thought. It would be hard to turn down, and yet she needed to. "I can't—"

"Please say yes," Tulip said, her voice almost urgent. "We really want you to come. Please."

She couldn't turn that strong plea down from a lady she'd come to admire hugely. "Okay, what time do I need to be ready and what type of clothes do I need to wear?"

"Great! We are going casual, so wear whatever you want. Jeans and a T-shirt, sandals or boots—whatever. We were hoping to leave in about an hour. Would that work?"

"Yes. I'm already dressed in that outfit, so I'll be ready whenever you want me to be."

"Wonderful. You never know…I'll pick them up and we might be there sooner."

"Okay, I'm sitting here drinking coffee, looking out the window, so I'll be watching for you." She hung up and a spike of happiness rose through her. This was what life would be like if she was able to somehow find a life with Austin. But would he be okay with her choice to keep her mouth shut about the jerk who had stolen all her money? Or would he insist she press charges and try to find the guy? If he insisted on that, could she do it— could she expose her stupidness like that? Then again, she knew she wasn't the only one who'd ever fallen for such a schemer. Some victims stood up and some just couldn't, and she didn't blame them because she was in their position. But because of that, she felt so low.

And not worthy of Austin.

She had finished her coffee, gone to the restroom and brushed her teeth, getting rid of the strong scent of coffee on her breath when they drove up in Tulip's black SUV. Seeing them drive up, her heart clenched then jumped with joy. She would so miss this wonderful group if she left. She had so much to lose if she didn't stand up for her rights. At least as much as she could, which, in most of the articles she'd read, were very hard to uphold. If you were dating them, they didn't always count it as scamming, and for her, she'd have to prove he got on her computer and into her checking account. It was a ridiculous situation she'd gotten herself into and now it was keeping her away from Austin.

She knew that if she walked away from Austin, who she was pretty sure loved her, she would never, ever fall in love again, or trust anyone. There was nothing about him not to trust. He had entire towns that supported him with love and wonderful things to say about him. He was wonderful. She just had to believe she was good enough for him.

And that was something that she couldn't believe in anymore.

All the windows of the SUV rolled down and all four of her friends were smiling at her: Tulip from the driver's seat, Hanna from the front passenger seat, and Ellie from the third seat in the back. Rita was across the aisle, in the second seat of the middle row where she would be sitting.

"Hop in," Tulip said with a big smile.

"Sure." She opened the door behind the passenger seat that Hanna was in and she climbed in.

Instantly, Ellie cupped her shoulder from the seat in the back. "We are so happy you're joining us."

"Yes, we are." Rita smiled from across the small space between them.

"This is going to be a great day," Hanna said, turning around and smiling. "We really are glad you decided to come with us."

A smiling Tulip looked at her very sincerely. "You have made our day, and we are going to try to make your day." With that, she backed out and drove out of the drive in the opposite direction of Fredericksburg.

She wasn't sure where they were going; maybe they were taking her to True Love for the day. But actually, she didn't care where they were going. In this moment, she felt better than she had felt all week, struggling over all the emotions she'd felt last weekend at the office fishing party and then spending the whole week worrying about what she needed to do. "I am really glad y'all called. I was really not going anywhere today; I just didn't want to be in the way." That completely didn't make sense, but it was all she could come up with at the moment.

"Why would our friend be in the way?" Hanna turned around in her seat again. "We are just out having fun, going antiques shopping and lunch. And hopefully have some visiting time."

"And it sounds really fun. I'm glad y'all wanted to invite me."

From that moment on, conversation went to what they'd each done that week. They weren't asking her questions, just including her. Hanna, the veterinarian, had had a bit of a rough week with several cattle problems, and also some dogs and cats owned by her in-town clients. There was a lot going on in her office and, thankfully, she'd said hiring another veterinarian had been the only reason she'd survived all the after-hours work that had gone on.

Tess had heard that Hanna was a wonderful vet, hardworking, and a very caring person and she believed every word just from the short time of knowing her.

Rita had taken some great pictures of several families and also the bridal shots of an upcoming wedding she and her other two sisters-in-law would be hosting. Rita was the photographer, Tulip was a yard designer and decorator, and Ellie was a florist. They all had their own business but loved the wedding parties and other big parties they could be hired to do. They had been a part of how she'd met Austin at Hanna and Jake's wedding, because they'd organized everything. If she hadn't been hired as a waitress and been watching that handsome doctor as he'd caught that garter while looking at her, she probably wouldn't have fallen. But that look in his eyes had just blown her feet out from under her. And then when she had opened her eyes and found his beautiful eyes staring down at her…her life had changed.

They passed through the tiny town of True Love, and they all asked her if she had visited other than driving through that night she'd come to dinner at the ranch with Austin.

"No, my time kind of disappeared from me and on my weekends off, I just stick around my tiny house. I haven't really thought about visiting the cute little town. It looks like a good place to visit. True Love—what a great name."

Ellie leaned forward, smiling, her eyes twinkling. "It's a magic name because it's true. True love happened here for all of us. And we are grateful that it did. We talk about it all the time. You know, all of us except me actually, were brought together after the men caught a garter at the wedding. The other three were the first woman their gaze fell on after catching the garter. Not me…I wasn't even at the wedding but came in later. But I've been amazed by the stories and believe the garter had something to do with their love stories. The garter brought them together."

"So true," said the others.

Austin had caught the garter too, while watching her, and she knew this from that night at the dinner with all of them. Their gazes had been so expectant that night at what they believed would happen between her and Austin. *Oh, how she did not need to think about that right now.*

"Anyway," Rita said. "We are a family, and we've been thoroughly pleased about it."

Hanna turned and grinned. "All right, enough about us falling in love because of a garter. Now, the town we're going to is just a little tiny place hidden back in here, but it has a wonderful diner overlooking the river and a couple of small antiques or junk stores, if you prefer to call it that. We all love exploring. I am looking for a couple of chairs to put at the front entrance of my clinic."

"And I'm looking for anything that grabs my attention," Rita said. "The new house is almost done and I am looking for many things. You'll have to come out and look. We are so excited."

"I would love to."

Conversation continued and then they rounded a corner of the road and came into the small town on the river. The Dancing Diner sign was the first thing she saw on the right side of the road, and then she saw a few places along the boardwalk, including the stores they were going to. It was a cute little town. People walked around, smiling and obviously having a good time. It was going to be a fun, relaxing day. A day she needed before she made a life-changing decision tonight or tomorrow.

* * *

"We weren't expecting you to come out and help herd cattle today." Bret glanced over from his horse as Austin rode up, his surprise clear in his gaze.

Austin had known his brothers were going to be surprised. He had just been too crazed up when he woke up this morning, and considering it was Saturday, he needed a distraction. He'd wanted to go find the creep who had messed up Tess's life, so he'd come to herd cattle instead. He'd come out to the ranch, saddled up and then texted them to find out where they were herding. Once he knew, he'd set his horse to a fast pace to catch up.

"Now that I'm not at the emergency room at all hours like I used to be, I get to do this every once in a while—even if I moved to the other ranch."

His brother hiked a brow. "Especially when you need an escape?"

"Yeah, you've got me pinned down. Absolutely right."

Cole rode up. "What's he got you pinned with?"

Bret looked from Austin to Cole as Levi and Jake rode up.

"What's going on?" Jake asked.

"Yeah, this is a surprise," Levi added. "And all of you look upset."

"Look." Austin sighed. "I came out to help y'all herd cattle."

Cole's expression hardened. "What were you saying to Bret when I rode up? Did it have something to do with Tess?"

He hadn't heard such demand in his older brother's voice in a very long time. "Fine, Bret guessed how I feel about Tess. That I love her."

They all looked at one another then at him. "We know that," they all said in a wave of the same words.

"If you love her, then why are you here?" Jake asked.

"Because there's more…it was a private thing, but I can't go on with it anymore. She dated a man before her mom and dad died who stole every cent she had from her bank account and savings, and then he disappeared. She had to move home, and then her parents had their car crash. Y'all know about that. Her mom died instantly, and her dad lasted a month. She was very grateful she was there for him." He yanked his hat off and rubbed the straw with both of his thumbs. He hadn't been able to hold it in any longer and wasn't sure Cole had, either, all this time. But the look on his other brothers' faces, learning the boyfriend had stolen all her money, told him Cole had kept his secret.

These were his brothers, and if anyone could give him good advice, it was them. He had to make sure his thoughts were right. He looked at Cole, who nodded at him. "I need advice. She doesn't want to go after this man. I had started investigating it, looking for him, but stopped after I told her what I was doing and she got so upset last Friday in my office. I think she was still upset with me about it on Saturday at the fishing event. Now, I have a fear she's going to quit at the office and run away and hide once more."

"Why?" Levi spoke up before the others could.

"Because she just wants to move on. He's probably used all her money, so she wouldn't get anything from it. And other things are against her—trying to prove he stole it, for one. And finding him. I understand her wanting to just move forward and try to forget it, but I think later, after she's had time, she'll regret it."

"I'm like you," Jake said. "I'd have a hard time not hunting the man down. But if he's like some of those fellas you see articles about sometimes, they use fake names and identification and do the same thing to a lot of people. It's terrible online but still happens in person too."

That his brother knew so much shocked Austin.

"How do you know all that? I just found it out since falling for Tess."

"I read an article about it on my phone from the local news channel and was so surprised, I looked it up and read several things. Probably the same things you've read."

"You're probably right. So what do all of you think I should do?"

Cole was first to speak. "I'd do what Tulip wanted if it was her, but tell her when she changed her mind, I was prepared to go all out to find and prosecute the piece of crap dude."

"I agree with Cole," Jake said. "Being by Hanna's side and having her love would be most important to me. And being there to protect her if the time came."

His other two brothers agreed, and Austin had his answer. "This is why I stopped the detective work, but I've just been torn, thinking I was doing the wrong thing for her. I love her and want to protect her, and if she leaves because she's afraid I'm going to ignore her wishes, then I lose everything."

His brothers all nodded with serious expressions on

their faces, telling him they had not given their answers without deep consideration. "Okay, then, I have my answer. Now I have to go tell her."

Cole held his hand up. "Not so fast. The ladies were calling her and going to get her to go to lunch and shopping. But Tulip said it was really to try to dig deeper to find out what is bothering her. They don't know this about the ex-boyfriend. They know about him but not the important stuff. So maybe find her later when she gets home. If she talks to the ladies, maybe it will help."

"Okay, sounds good. I'll ride with y'all for a bit, then head back to be ready when she gets home. I really love all of you and your spouses. Tess fits right in."

CHAPTER FIFTEEN

Tess walked out of the resale store, smiling, as her favorite friends walked out beside her. "That was so fun. And I'm glad you found those beautiful candlesticks, Rita."

"Thanks. I am, too. They'll be perfect on my fireplace mantel."

"Okay, it's time to eat." Tulip grinned. "I called and had them hold the table that's by itself, down the stairs. It's going to be perfect."

Everyone got excited and Tess was really curious to see the spot. Instead of going inside the diner, they went along the path that led around the edge of the building. She saw the river and it had a patio that was surprisingly large, overlooking the flowing water. It also had stairs that led down to a few decks with tables, and there was a spot off to the right in a cute section, all alone. She had a feeling that it was theirs.

"This is wonderful," she said to everyone. "I would have never guessed from the front look of this little café that this beautiful place was back here. It's amazing."

Hanna smiled hugely. "I know. I was the same way the first time I came here. And I still come here with Jake whenever we have time. We love it. The chicken strawberry salad is amazing."

The waitress came up and Tulip told them they had a reservation under the name Tanner. They were led to the table down the steps, off to the side that she'd noticed, and they all took a seat. After they gave their drink orders, they were left alone to glance around and enjoy the view.

"It's a lovely place," she said.

"We thought you'd like it," Tulip said.

They all chatted about the view and the food as they looked over the menu. The waitress brought their drinks and took their orders of the strawberry chicken salads they'd all decided to order, then left. It was then that they all looked at one another and suddenly it dawned on her that there had been more to the trip than she'd realized.

"Okay, Tess," Tulip said. "I asked the others to join me here with you because I'm concerned that something really serious is bothering you. Last weekend, you seemed happy and then after you and Austin raced together, which looked like y'all were enjoying it when I glanced over at you, you were different after that. But when we helped you clean up, you didn't say much and then you left. We've really been worried. And he hasn't acted normal either, the little bit that we see him now. We used to see him almost every evening when he headed to the cabin but now that he's at the new place, it's different. But the guys go over there and herd cattle, and I asked Cole if he'd noticed anything about his brother and he said yes. And that he was worried."

"See, because he has been very happy since he met you," Ellie added.

Hanna and Rita agreed.

Her internal emotions sank, not with anger but instead with love. These girls, these four wonderful ladies cared for her. And she hadn't had that in so very long. The fact that they did all of this today just to have this conversation with her after having fun with her shopping filled her with joy that she needed desperately. Her hand trembled on her drink that she'd reached for; she took it off and laid her hand on the table. Instantly, all of them covered her hand with their hands piled on top of each other. She looked around the table and a tear rolled down the side of her face. She did not need to cry. She didn't…but the look on Rita's, Hanna's, Ellie's, and Tulip's faces was truly of caring and concern.

"I have a problem," she offered. "And it concerns my life here in town and what my heart is wishing for…a life with Austin. A life that I don't know will come to fruition if I don't face up to something."

"Please tell us," Ellie urged.

"Yes, please," Tulip agreed. "We love you and feel like you fit with us. We feel like you and Austin were meant for each other. And not just because he caught the garter at Jake and Hanna's wedding. Even if he hadn't, you would have been like Bret and Ellie, meant for each other. But even if you and Austin don't end up together, you are our friend. And we want to help you with this situation."

"We really do," Hanna offered. "You are an awesome lady who stepped in where you were needed. Even after you were hurt at that wedding of ours. You just make us think you need to talk, and we are here for you."

"I agree totally," Rita added. "We are here for you. Please trust us. We so want to help you. You lost your parents and then you are here, and other than joining in with us, you haven't seemed to reach out much. But we are here for you."

"If you trust us," Tulip added.

Tess knew in that moment after they'd all spoken that they were exactly what she needed. They all removed their hands from hers, and she picked up her glass of water and set it down. "The man I dated before I moved home with Mom and Dad was horrible in what he did to me, but it got me home, where I needed to be because I was soon to lose them. Being home enabled me to spend time with them for a short while before they were taken from me. But him…what he did to me still affects my future, and I don't really know what to do about it." She paused and took a breath.

They all did, too, but they remained silent, giving her time to continue. But their expressions were clearly sincere with wanting to help her.

She picked up a napkin and dabbed at the moisture in her eyes. "He was one of those men you read about who steals from the woman they are dating. He was one of the ones who stole as much as he could. He got into my account after seeing it the night before when he came over and I was making out checks and also paying accounts online. He stole not only my money in my checking account, but also my savings. At least, that's what I believe. The account it was all sent to was just as quickly closed."

They all looked horrified.

"What did you do?" Rita asked.

"I did go to the police but they told me I didn't have a good case after having shown him my account and because we had been dating for a few weeks. They said it would be hard to bring him down and it could cost me a lot of money to do it. I left there soon after, and didn't file anything. I just couldn't do it. I couldn't admit to anyone what I'd done. Especially knowing I was probably not getting anything back and it was more than likely going to cost me money I didn't have, and the chances of him walking away a free man were high.

"I moved from Houston back home with my parents since I had no money for my rent. They were so upset but my mom thought I'd made the right decision to just start over. She didn't think they'd have found enough to put the man in prison if they ever figured out what his real name was. She felt like I was going to put my name out there, it'd cost me money and that he would walk free. And my dad was torn with what was best but his last words to me were: live a good life.

"I spent the next little while after he died trying to make sure what they had in their accounts was used to pay off their bills. When it was over, there wasn't much at all left over, even with the sell of their small home and the hospital bills getting paid. I loved them so much…I used to be stronger than I am now. Meeting y'all and meeting Austin especially made me more like who I used to be. But that lingering feeling of not being worthy of a man like Austin drives me to not tell him how I feel.

"And he knows all this, and he wants to hunt him down. I told him, no, I can't do that. I still haven't had the desire after losing my mom and dad and seeing how short life can be sometimes…I can't convince myself to spend the rest of my life looking for this horrible person. Instead, I'd like to just move forward, but I don't think Austin could do that. He's very heroic and he wants to help my life get better."

"He loves you," Hanna said. "But he has to understand where you are coming from. You have to tell him what you've told us, let him see your emotions and exactly how you feel. And you need to tell him how you feel about him. It doesn't sound like y'all have opened up about that to each other. Am I right?"

All the other friends watched her but said nothing.

"Yes, you're right. We've never completely expressed how we feel about each other. He may not—"

"He does," Tulip broke in. "You can see his love in his eyes, hear it in his voice when he talks about you."

"That is so true," Rita agreed. "He lights up."

"He does," Ellie said softly. "He loves you. Please don't run away. Don't leave us. We know what happened and we hugely want to support you in whatever you want to do about this pathetic piece of junk who did this to you. But remember you have a marvelous, strong man who loves you and is just waiting. I guess I said that wrong. You two really need to talk this out and figure it out together."

Tess took a deep breath, knowing what they'd all said was true. She could not run away anymore.

* * *

Austin got home after lunch and showered quickly. His mind was reeling with what his next step should be…it was time to tell her that his heart belonged to her. And to hope she said the same. He had texted Tulip to find out when they were taking Tess home, and he parked down the road and waited for them to drive back by, heading home. After they passed back by, he drove to Tess's and parked his truck. Determined, he got out, closed his door, and strode to the door and knocked. He said a quick prayer for the right words.

Moments later, the door opened, and the love of his life stared in shock at him. She was beautiful and he so wanted this situation between them to work out. He was willing to do whatever it took to make it do exactly that.

"Austin, hello. Wh-what are you doing?"

"I came to see if you would go for a ride with me. I think we should talk."

She shifted from one foot to the other, looking hesitant but also deep in thought. "Yes, I think we do need to talk. I just got back from shopping with all of your sisters-in-law, and we had a great time. I knew we needed to talk but after spending time with them, I knew it needed to be soon and here you are. Let me grab my purse and shades. Do you want to come in or wait there?"

"Here," he said. But when she walked away, he needed to move, so he went to the truck and opened the passenger door. She was back in a moment, locked her front door and then came and climbed into the seat. He had resisted the urge to reach and help her in, because at the moment, he did not need to touch her. He would pull her too close. So he kept his hands to himself as he closed the door then hurried around to his side, got in and backed out.

"Where are we going?" she asked.

"I was thinking we would drive out to the ranch. Maybe we could talk there. Not at the ranch house but at the lake."

"That sounds good."

On the way, she told him about the little town she and the others had gone to. She had loved it but especially the restaurant with the wonderful outdoor seating and delicious chicken salad. It sounded great. He'd heard his brothers mention it too.

"Maybe one day I can take you out there and we can sit and enjoy the scene and eat that salad you liked so much."

"That would be nice. I didn't buy anything, just ate. I'm concentrating on every penny I have to build up my savings and starting over. It feels good, getting my feet back on the ground."

He so wanted to point out that if she loved him and agreed to marry him like he wanted to ask her, that she'd be able to do whatever she wanted to do. But he was not using his money to try to bring her to him; he didn't think she'd appreciate such an offer anyway. This was strictly about them, and their feelings toward each other.

At least, he hoped that was what it was about. And he felt sure of that because she never asked for anything. She worked hard at what she did and was expectant of herself. And he knew, given the chance, she would highly succeed. She'd helped him out so much in his office that he would hate to lose her but even more, he hated even the thought that he could lose her for the rest of his life.

He turned down the main lane onto his property but instead of heading toward the house, he drove toward the lake. But instead of driving down to the area the fishing had been held, he headed around to the other side. On that side, there was a pier and he'd set a couple of wooden chairs on the pier. He parked and glanced at her. "Will this work? I don't think it will be too hot."

"It's great. Just enough breeze blowing, and I can use some sun."

"Great." He got out and headed around to help her

out but she was already out and closing her door when he arrived. He reached in the backseat instead and pulled out a picnic basket. "Just some drinks and snacks in case we want something. And if you need to go to the restroom, I'll run you over to the house."

She smiled. "I've already done that and should last at least a couple of hours, if we're here that long."

He grinned, teasing about the bathroom matter. They walked over to the pier and as they walked down it, he wanted so badly to drape an arm on her shoulders and pull her close. But he knew first they had to talk. He hoped that after that, she would want him to hold her forever and not leave him like he'd been fearing she was going to do.

"This is a beautiful lake," Tess said when they reached the end of the pier, where it widened and the chairs sat. She looked over the huge stretch of lake. "It's pretty from the other side but this view is the best. You're looking over the water then down the hill and can see the road out there. I really like it."

He set the basket down between the chairs and stuffed his fingers in the pockets of his jeans to keep them where they belonged. "I think so too. When I build the house, it will be here, just back a bit from the water. Of course, when me and my wife have children, we'll have to do a lot of watching and teaching them to swim in case at some point they do fall in, but it's very doable."

Her eyes had softened as she looked from the water to the area where the house would be, and then she looked at him. His heart raged with longing and hope.

"You're going to be a great father, and you'll do what is right by your children."

"Thank you, and I can say the same for you, as a mother that is."

She hefted her left shoulder slightly. "Maybe. Anyway, what did we come out here for?"

He pointed to her chair. "Please have a seat." She did what he asked and he took the one beside her that was slightly angled so they could see each other better. "I have to tell you that I'm sorry about what I said at our last meeting in my office. To be honest with you, and if you haven't guessed it already, I love you. I can't not tell you anymore. I have no idea if you're going to stick around any longer since we had different feelings about the man who did you wrong. But I do know how much I love you.

"I have talked—I hope you don't mind, because I needed a little confirmation that I'm not doing the wrong thing—so I talked with my brothers. Please don't hate me. I told them about the guy who stole your money. I had already come to the decision I'm about to tell you and they all agreed with me. I love you, and whatever you decide to do to that man is your business. I'm here for you. I want to be in your life. I want you to love me and marry me. It's a terrible way to be asking you but the option needs to be out there so you'll know how deeply I care for you. I fear if I drop down on my knee before we have this talk that you would tell me no. But I need you to understand where I'm coming from.

"I love you and I don't want to dictate your life. I wasn't there when he did that to you, and I realized finally that I can't determine your path about what he did to you. All I can offer you is that I love you. I want to be with you, to support you in whichever way you want to go in this situation and all situations. With all my heart, I hope that you love me. And if I don't pressure you to do anything about that guy, since it's your decision to make, I hope you might want to spend the rest of your life with me…the man who wants to be your support, lover, lifelong love.

"I didn't get all that said the other day. I was just so mad that the guy did that to you and all I could think about was finding him and bringing him down. But, like you, I realized that that's not always easy and it could expose you to more trauma and no justice in the end, so I get it. My main want is to be here beside you, loving you and protecting you if that creep ever returns for any reason into your life. I just want to love you, hold you, and have you by my side forever."

He paused, his heart thundering. He had talked and talked, and she had just watched him. Her expression had gone blank, then pale, and then her eyes had brightened with tears. And now, she had a very small, faint smile at the corners of her mouth. His hopes sparked as he waited for her to speak.

"I…love you, Austin. I have loved you from almost the beginning, though I was in denial and wouldn't let my mind go there after what had happened to me. Are you sure me not going after that horrible man won't turn you away? Because, right now, all I want is for you to love me. I want to forget him and what he did. But maybe later, after I've relaxed in my happiness with you, I'll also decide that I have the strength to speak out."

Without hesitating, he stood, reached down, and took her hand then pulled her into his arms and kissed the top of her head. He embraced her against him, and she pressed her cheek against his heart. He looked up at the sky and thanked God for this wonderful woman who had filled his life with everything he needed, and now he could be devoted to doing the same thing for her. She leaned her head back and he dropped his lips to hers.

But right before he kissed her, he said, "You have filled my life with joy. I can't wait to build this house with you, and be there with you in any way that you want. I love you." And then he kissed her. Softly at first, then her arms tightened around him and he felt a tear on her cheek against his cheek. He deepened the kiss as her hands tightened more, pulling him closer and he gladly increased his hold on her.

Too quickly, she pulled back. "I have never been happier in all of my life. You are what I've been waiting on, Austin, and we are going to have a wonderful life together."

And then she lifted her face to his and kissed him again, and he had no complaints. He knew that guy was out there, and if she ever said let's go get him, they would.

But right now, it was about each other, and he was all in…and if it had anything to do with him catching that garter at his brother's wedding and meeting Tess's gaze, then he was forever grateful for that odd but wonderful moment in life.

More Books by Hope Moore

McCoy Billionaire Brothers
Her Billionaire Cowboy's Fake Marriage
Her Billionaire Cowboy's Fake Wedding Fiasco
Her Billionaire Cowboy's Trouble in Paradise
Her Billionaire Cowboy's Secret Baby Surprise
Her Billionaire Cowboy's Second Chance Romance
Her Billionaire Cowboy Fake Fiancé
Her Billionaire Cowboy's Inconvenient Marriage Blessing

Billionaire Cowboys of True Love, Texas
Billionaire Cowboy's Runaway Bride
Billionaire Cowboy's Wedding Crasher
Her Billionaire Cowboy's Hill Country Proposal
Billionaire Cowboy Auctioned at Christmas
Billionaire Cowboy's Dream Come True

About the Author

Hope Moore is the pen name of an award-winning author who lives deep in the heart of Texas surrounded by Christian cowboys who give her inspiration for all of her inspirational sweet romances. She loves writing clean & wholesome, swoon worthy romances for all of her fans to enjoy and share with everyone. Her heartwarming, feel good romances are full of humor and heart, and gorgeous cowboys and heroes to love. And the spunky women they fall in love with and live happily-ever-after.

When she isn't writing, she's trying very hard not to cook, since she could live on peanut butter sandwiches, shredded wheat, coffee...and cheesecake why should she cook? She loves writing though and creating new stories is her passion. Though she does love shoes, she's admitted she has an addiction and tries really hard to stay out of shoe stores. She, however, is not addicted to social media and chooses to write instead of surf FB - but she LOVES her readers so she's working on a free novella just for you and if you sign up for her newsletter she will send it to you as soon as its ready! You'll also receive snippets of her adventures, along with special deals, sneak peaks of soon-to-be released books and of course any sales she might be having.

She promises she will not spam you, she hates to be spammed also, so she wouldn't dare do that to people she's crazy about (that means YOU). You can unsubscribe at any time.

Sign up for my newsletter:
www.subscribepage.com/hopemooresignup

I can't wait to hear from you.

Hope Moore~
Always hoping for more love, laughter and reading for you every day of your life!